DEADLY RAGE

The dim stable whirled, and darkness closed in on all sides as the pain from the blow radiated through his skull. Fargo felt his body falling through space, knew he was losing consciousness. The stable floor came flying toward him, hit hard, and he felt his body roll over as if from a far distance, heard a man laugh, and rage welled up in him, red and hot. Fury pounded in his blood. He felt his fists clench, the fingernails digging into his palm, the pain of that bringing him to clarity, fighting the enormous throb in his head.

"He's out cold," a voice said.

Someone, a dark figure, leaned over him, and he felt a hand fumbling, trying to remove his fingers from his gun. The rage welled up again, a gigantic wave that opened his eyes, and he pulled the barrel up in an instant, hard against the man's grasp, willed his mind to pull the trigger.

The Colt exploded, the gunfire rupturing the waves in his head. The dark figure looming over him staggered backward at the force of the bullet. . . .

BLACKGULCH GAMBLE

by

Jon Sharpe

SIGNET
Published by the Penguin Group
Penguin Putnam Inc., 375 Hudson Street,
New York, New York 10014, U.S.A.
Penguin Books Ltd, 27 Wrights Lane,
London W8 5TZ, England
Penguin Books Australia Ltd,
Ringwood, Victoria, Australia
Penguin Books Canada Ltd, 10 Alcorn Avenue,
Toronto, Ontario, Canada M4V 3B2
Penguin Books (N.Z.) Ltd, 182–190 Wairau Road,
Auckland 10, New Zealand

Penguin Books Ltd, Registered Offices:
Harmondsworth, Middlesex, England

First published by Signet, an imprint of Dutton NAL,
a member of Penguin Putnam Inc.

First Printing, June, 1998
10 9 8 7 6 5 4 3 2 1

The first chapter of this book originally appeared in *Utah Uprising*,
the one hundred ninety-seventh volume in this series.

Printed in the United States of America

The Trailsman

Beginnings . . . they bend the tree and they mark the man. Skye Fargo was born when he was eighteen. Terror was his midwife, vengeance his first cry. Killing spawned Skye Fargo, ruthless, cold-blooded murder. Out of the acrid smoke of gunpowder still hanging in the air, he rose, cried out a promise never forgotten.

The Trailsman they began to call him all across the West: searcher, scout, hunter, the man who could see where others only looked, his skills for hire but not his soul, the man who lived each day to the fullest, yet trailed each tomorrow. Skye Fargo, the Trailsman, and the seeker who could take the wildness of a land and the wanting of a woman and make them his own.

In 1860, on a high-stakes Mississippi riverboat,
or in a gambling Texas town called Blackgulch,
a man could find any crooked game he wanted
to play if he was willing to stake his gold,
his woman, and his life. . . .

1

"Lay down your bets, men! Three to one on the big red, three to one, now lay your bets!" A squat man in a green hat was moving through the crowd. "He's a champ-een, that big red. Going to be a bloody fight. Bloody, bloody fight to the finish! Three to one!"

The tall stranger with the dark beard paused and looked over the heads of the roiling throng gathered at dusk around a small fenced enclosure in the middle of the dockside street in New Orleans. Two men, each clutching a struggling rooster, eyed each other warily. The cocks' heads moved convulsively back and forth, their ruddy combs trembling, their beady eyes black. Around the birds' yellow legs were strapped razor-sharp spurs. Onlookers tossed coins and dollar bills into a box.

"Three to one, three to one on the big red! A real champ-een, one of the best! Get ready!" The green-hatted man shouldered his way toward the tall quiet stranger. "How about you, mister? Three to one! Take it from me and put it on the big red. Sure to win. Make you some fast bucks."

"Don't care for cockfights," the tall man mumbled as he pushed his way out of the crowd. His lake blue eyes scanned the New Orleans street. Along the row of brick buildings with lacy wrought-iron porches and stairways, streetlamps were being lit, golden flames sparkling in the glass globes. The sky above still held the light of sunset. The street was jammed with a restless moving horde that rushed and eddied like a tumultuous river.

The cacophony of voices, of shouts and cries was deafening. A roar welled up as the cockfight began and the crowd pressed against him, trying to get closer to the excitement. Off to his left, a dour fellow sat on the seat of a shebang and called out the prices of patent medicines. A thimble-rigger tried to get suckers to put down quarters as he deftly moved small thimbles across a felt-covered table, lifting one from time to time to show the joker, a little white pebble, underneath. Another man called out an advertisement for new boots while a rotund woman offered glasses of draft beer from the back of a wagon for twenty cents a mug. A band of street musicians stood on a wrought-iron porch and played trumpets, drums, and flutes, but he could only catch an occasional strain of melody amidst all the ruckus.

New Orleans was a jambalaya stew of every kind of person imaginable, Skye Fargo thought to himself. A swarthy couple passed by, their dark wavy hair and colorfully ribboned clothes marking them as Creole. There were mulattoes from Jamaica, a German fellow in a feather hat, a couple of pretty Italian women, a cockney fresh from St. Giles, from the sound of his accent. Three tanned Aussies who looked like ex-convicts rough-housed as they made their way along the street. A lone Celestial in a conical hat and long pigtail slipped by like a shadow. A knot of Cherokee Indians with blanketed shoulders stood watching the auctioneer. Some Kanakas from Hawaii and a strong black man carried crates on their shoulders. Peruvians played pan pipes and beat on drums. A Mexican family in brightly striped cloth stood watching the cockfight.

The wild and steamy city of New Orleans was a crossroads. From here, a man traveled across the gulf to the southern islands or out across the vast expanse of land toward the western frontier or northward up the broad highway of the river.

Beyond the crowd, Fargo glimpsed the muddy brown Mississippi, wide as a lake and seemingly motionless. A flock of ships anchored just offshore waved high masts against the peachblow clouds, like a forest of swaying trees. A long dock jutted out into the water. He looked up the river but saw no sign of the paddleboat, the *Lady Luck*. When would it arrive? The sunset was just fading. Maybe another hour, he thought. Around about nightfall, they had said. He'd just finished a job and had a big wad of cash pushed deep into an inner pocket of his jacket. He could use a rest, he'd decided. A hot bath every day, good food, fine brandy, some female company. So he'd decided a week on a gambling riverboat paddling up the Mississippi would cure him of his itch for the comforts of civilization. For a while anyway. And the *Lady Luck* was reputed to be one of the most luxurious riverboats on the river.

Fargo spotted a gleaming white standing-top phaeton drawn by two snowy horses and driven by an old man in a frock coat. The open carriage was inching through the packed street. But what attracted his attention was the woman who sat inside. Her gleaming dark hair was piled high, stuck with a red ostrich feather that fluttered each time she turned her head. Below her jewel-wound neck, her scarlet gown was cut daringly low to reveal mounds of generous breasts and deep cleavage. She seemed to be looking for something out on the river. He pushed his way through the mob until he was within ten feet of her. She happened to glance back and catch his gaze.

Her eyes were the startling color of cornflowers, almost pale purple, fringed with thick dark lashes, punctuated by dramatically arched brows. For all the sophistication of her dress, there seemed to be a kind of innocence in her eyes, almost a naive surprise. She smiled, rose-dimpled, as her eyes held his for a brief moment. Then she tugged at the driver's coat. He halted and she rose to get out of the carriage.

Fargo elbowed his way toward her and offered his hand. She took it and stepped out. She was short, just reaching his broad chest. He bent down slightly and put his lips to her ear. The din was so loud, he practically had to shout.

"You looking for the *Lady Luck* too?"

She seemed surprised at the question and pulled back, looking at him suspiciously. She nodded hesitantly.

"I figured as much. I saw you looking toward the river," he explained. "I'm waiting for the same riverboat."

Her lips formed a silent *Oh* and she nodded. He started to ask her name but she swiftly raised one hand as if bidding him good-bye.

"I suppose I'll see you on board," she called out stiffly and turned her back, making her way through the crowd.

Fargo swore to himself and watched her go. There was no understanding women. He watched other men turn to admire her as she slipped among them. She'd hardly got five yards through the throng when the three Aussies bumped into her. They were an unsavory lot, unshaven and mean-looking. He'd noticed them before—they sure looked like ex-convicts. And now they'd noticed the woman in red and saw she was unaccompanied.

Although he couldn't hear their words over the hubbub, Fargo could imagine what the three men were saying as they suddenly surrounded her. She turned about in a swirl of crimson, her expression puzzled, then angry, then frightened. He could tell even through the crowd, the men were making a grab for her. Fargo shoved his way toward them, closer and closer. They had her surrounded and were hustling her toward a dark alley. She was struggling, her mouth open in a scream but in the blaring commotion, she couldn't be heard. No one was taking notice.

In a few swift strides, Fargo caught up to them, reached out a strong arm and grabbed a collar, suddenly hauling one of the men backward. The man lost his balance and whirled about, surprise on his grizzled face. Fargo swung a whistling left that snapped his head half around and the man's eyes rolled back as he crumpled into a heap. The crowd eddied around them. The second man, tall and broad, pushed the woman behind him and brought up his fists. Fargo lashed out again, but the man stepped backward, then struck, a stinging right to Fargo's belly. Fargo swore at the pain and ducked a sizzling left that whistled through the air, then balled his rock-hard fist and drove it upward into the tall man's jaw. His head snapped back just as Fargo felt a kick against his leg that barely missed his groin. The third man, short and stocky, had come about. The tall man was staggering and Fargo followed with another drive, a powerful left into his midsection. The tall man gasped for air like a fish and his knees gave way. Just then, Fargo felt an electric shock along his jaw, followed by dancing stars, and the crowd scene began to whirl. The third man had delivered a near-knockout punch. Fargo gritted his teeth and the short man's face swam in front of his eyes as if in a dream and the man's fist was heading toward his face. With a shout of rage, Fargo pulled up his fists in a lightning fast motion, blocked the punch, and drove hard, smashing once, twice, a third time into the short man's head.

In a moment, it was over and the last man went down. Fargo took a deep breath and shook his head to clear it, rubbed his face, and felt the bruise and swelling along the jaw. Nothing broken. He looked around for the woman in red, expecting to see her there. He turned, looked behind him, and scanned the swirling crowd. But she was gone. Well, that figured.

He moved away from the spot before the three troublemakers could come to their senses. The sunset had faded completely, the evening stars were out, and the golden-flamed lamps glimmered in the blue dusk all along the crowded street. Fargo pushed his way toward the side street that led to the stables where he'd left the Ovaro. He might as well fetch the pinto down to the dock, ready to board, since the *Lady Luck* would be coming along any time now. He'd reserved the best stateroom on board and had made arrangements for the pinto to be transported on deck. Yeah, he was looking forward to this trip.

As he rounded the corner, he came to a narrow alley behind the stables and noticed a rear door. It was ajar and he walked in. The warm odor of hay and animals enveloped him. Inside it was dark with only one oil lamp lit in the distance, at the main entrance. He heard men's voices, at least a dozen, but couldn't quite make out the words. He started to walk forward, then something in their tone—an urgency, a secrecy—made him stop, melt into the shadow along the line of stalls, and ease forward until he could make out what they were saying.

"So, did you even spot her?" one said.

"In that crowd? You gotta be kidding." It was a gravelly voice, low and distinctive.

"Well, we know she always wears red. That should make it easy."

"Yeah, real easy. There's a thousand women out there in red dresses tonight. I told you this was a harebrained idea."

Fargo crept closer until he was just at the edge of the light. At least a dozen men, maybe more, stood by the open doors. It was too dark to see any faces.

"All right, all right. Keep your shirt on."

"Even if we see her, we're not going to be able to do anything." It was the gravel-voiced one again. "So what if we find her? What are we going to do about it? Grab her right in the middle of the street? There's a thousand people around all the time."

"All right, all right. At least we found out she's traveling on the *Lady Luck*. That's all we need. There's nothing more we can do here. Let's go catch up with the others."

Fargo stood motionless against the stall as the shadowy men saddled up and led their horses from the stable. He heard the creak of leather as they mounted, the clop of hooves on cobblestones as they rode away. He waited until the last sound faded. Then he went to the Ovaro's stall. The black-

and-white pinto nuzzled him. He lit a lamp and began saddling the horse. All the while, he was preoccupied by what the mysterious men had said. Were they talking about the same woman in red? He didn't like what he'd heard. It sounded like she was heading for trouble. Big trouble. He was leading the Ovaro out the front door and into the street when he heard the crackle of footsteps. The hunchbacked stablemaster was hobbling toward him as fast as he could.

"Hold up, Mr. Fargo!" the old man said, panting. He paused and held on to the side of the pinto's saddle as he gasped and caught his breath. "Got a message for you. Must be important. I said I'd get it to you for sure."

The old man pulled an envelope out of his jacket and handed it over. Fargo moved toward the oil lamp and turned it over in his hands. The thick envelope was postmarked Arizona a few weeks ago. He'd been in Arizona about a month before.

"It must be real important," the old man repeated. "The man who delivered it said they've been trying to track you down for a long long time."

Fargo tore open the envelope, but instead of a message, he found another envelope inside. This was postmarked Nevada. Yeah, he'd been there recently too. The third envelope was from Wyoming and the fourth from Montana. Whatever the message was, it had been trailing him for a while but never quite caught up. Finally, inside the last envelope, he found the message, a telegram that had been sent to Denver City from Blackgulch three months before. And that was all that was clear. The rest was a bunch of meaningless letters bunched together. Unreadable. Someone had written across it, "Garbled in Transmission. Correction requested but no reply. Denver City Telegraph Office."

The old man was looking over his arm, trying to read the message.

"Looks like some kind of code," the stablemaster said, impressed.

"Nah, it's just a mess," Fargo said. Great. There was no way to tell what the message was supposed to say. He didn't have a clue who had sent it. He examined it again. *Blackgulch.* That was the one word he could read. But Blackgulch where? He shook his head. There were probably a dozen rinky-dink towns called Blackgulch out in the western territories. There was no telling where the message had come from. Whoever sent it had probably given up on him by now—three months was a long time. He folded up the message along with the envelopes and tucked them in his inside vest pocket, bid the stablemaster good-bye and led the pinto away.

As he turned onto the thronged dockside street, out on the river he spotted the glistening ivory boat called the *Lady Luck.* She was a beautiful sight, steaming straight toward the dock. Her wide white bow was reflected on the muddy water like a grand lady with a hoop skirt gliding across a polished ballroom floor. Her two smokestacks puffed gray clouds against the stars, the paddle slapped the river, and the three gingerbread balconies sparkled with golden torches. Across the water, he could hear strains of music and the vivacious laughter of the men and women on board. Fargo led the pinto out onto the long wooden dock.

The woman in red stood looking out at the approaching riverboat. Beside her loomed a small mountain of red leather luggage. Fargo walked up beside her and touched the brim of his hat as her wide cornflower eyes blinked up at him, startled.

"Oh. Oh—you again," she said. Her black eyebrows arched and she turned her attention to the oncoming *Lady Luck*.

"Pretty cool welcome to someone who got those three bruisers off you," he said, feeling a bit hot under the collar. She looked up at him again and her expression softened.

"Forgive me," she said then with a smile. "I'm being thoughtless. Of course. Thank you for what you did back there. Forgive me?" She laid a light hand on his arm. Her lashes were dark and long fringes around her eyes. Those eyes. Just how innocent was she? Never mind. She was beautiful anyway. He grinned down at her and introduced himself.

"And I'm Ruby Murphy." She offered her hand.

"Got some bad news for you," he said. And he told her about what he'd overheard in the stables. When he'd finished, she burst into a merry laugh.

"But that's absurd! I have no idea who those men were. They must have been talking about somebody else. Nobody's coming after me. The whole thing's ridiculous!"

"You can't think of anybody who might be looking for you?"

"Not a soul!" Ruby said without hesitation.

"Well, you ought to watch out anyhow."

"Or have somebody watch out for me, I bet you mean." Ruby glanced at him out of the corners of her eyes. "Why, Mr. Fargo, I've rarely heard a man make up such a foolish story just to try to scare a woman into thinking she needs his protection. Nobody is looking for me. Except maybe you, of course. And I am perfectly able to take care of myself."

"I'll remember that next time I see three men try to drag you off," he said. He'd had enough. Ruby Murphy was beautiful but she was also too difficult and stubborn. If she wasn't going to take his advice, then to hell with her. He turned away and led the pinto to a point close to the boarding ramp. He could feel her eyes on him but he'd be damned if he'd look back. Instead, he turned his attention to the several horses waiting to be boarded. A spectacular Arabian horse stood nearby. It was one of the finest mounts he'd seen, after the Ovaro, of course. The Arabian's long legs and slender neck marked it as a thoroughbred with a lot of speed, but it also had the powerful chest and strong haunches that would make it a steed with great endurance.

The man holding the Arabian's bridle was smallish, wiry. He was dressed in a walnut homespun shirt, stained leather breeches, and battered boots that had seen better days. The man noticed Fargo's attention and doffed his hickory slouch hat. Everything about him was brown—his thick ragged-cut hair, his crookedly trimmed mustache, his worn complexion. He looked like a country rube, the kind of man who made his way by taking on odd jobs and doing some trapping and trading. An unusual owner for such an expensive horse.

"Fine horse," Fargo said appreciatively.

"Yours too," the man responded with a friendly smile as he eyed the black-and-white pinto.

"Don't see many Arabians around. Must have cost a pretty penny."

"Didn't cost a nickel," the man in brown responded with a laugh as if abashed. "I just got lucky in a coin toss one day. The name's Josh Leatherberry."

"Skye Fargo."

"Why, you're the one folks call the Trailsman," Leatherberry said, his face wrinkling with surprise. "Well, I'm sure glad to meet you."

"So you won that horse with a coin toss? You always have that kind of luck?"

"Hell no," Leatherberry said, his face open and bemused. "I'd say till I won this horse, I'd never been lucky in my life. Just a hardworking man trying to get by. Anyhow, Mr. Fargo," he went on as if eager to change the subject, "I've heard a lot about you over the years and I'm glad to finally meet you." Leatherberry stuck out his hand.

As they shook, Fargo felt a wave of surprise. Josh

Leatherberry's hand was as soft and narrow as a woman's, his fingers smooth as silk with nary a callous. Hardly the kind of hands Fargo had expected on such a rough-looking man. Nevertheless, he kept the surprise off his face. There was obviously more to Josh Leatherberry than first met the eye.

Just then, with a jolt and a scraping of wood on wood, the *Lady Luck* pulled up alongside the dock. Three men jumped off and made her fast with ropes as the gangplank was lowered. Women in bright colors and gambling men in their brocade vests and waxed mustaches began to disembark. After a few minutes, the passengers were all off and the trunks and crates unloaded. A crowd of travelers had gathered, waiting to get on board. Fargo saw an elderly black man with silvery hair standing at the top of the gangplank.

"All aboard!" he called out. "*Lady Luck* now boarding passengers for the trip to St. Louie. All aboard!"

The woman in red swept up the gangplank first, her tall ostrich feather fluttering. A couple of crew members scurried behind carrying her red leather bags. A swarm of other travelers, professional gamblers and their doves by the looks of them, followed.

"You down there! You with the horses!" the black man was calling out. "Get ready to board."

"Why are you going up to St. Louie?" Fargo asked casually as he and Leatherberry brought their steeds toward the gangplank. He was more and more curious about the strange man in brown with the Arabian horse.

"Oh, I never been on a gamblin' boat before," Leatherberry said with a shrug. "But when I won this here Araby horse, I thought maybe luck was running with me. Don't really know anything about cards and all. But this past winter, I made a good piece of money trapping some beaver and I thought I'd put it down on the tables and see if my luck would stay with me."

Fargo nodded affably, thinking of the man's smooth hands that had not recently—if ever—tied a buckskin thong on a trap, or hacked through ice with a broadax, or scraped flesh off beaverskin. Josh Leatherberry was telling a lie for sure. He was no more a trapper than he was a dance-hall girl. Well, whatever Leatherberry's story really was, he was a man to keep an eye on. He felt curiosity prick him. But, he told himself, for one whole week he was just going to relax and enjoy himself.

He led the Ovaro clopping up the gangplank and Leatherberry followed with the Arabian. At the top, they were met by the elderly black man.

"I'm Sims, Steward of the *Lady Luck*," the man said, his brown eyes flashing. He consulted a piece of paper in his hand. "You gentlemen must be Mr. Fargo and Mr. Leatherberry. Now, just bring your horses this way."

Sims led the way along the deck toward the rear, where a small wooden shelter stood back by the paddle wheel. Inside were several stalls filled with hay. Fargo made sure the Ovaro would have plenty of feed and water.

"Now, Mr. Fargo, I'll take you to your state-room," Sims said. "You'll be staying in the presidential suite. And, Mr. Leatherberry, I see that you've booked passage to sleep on deck."

Leatherberry, busy unsaddling the Arabian, nodded.

"Some of us got to save money and ain't quite so fancy," he said with a grin at Fargo. There was no envy or malice in it and Fargo found himself liking Josh Leatherberry, despite the air of mystery around his circumstances.

"See you around," Fargo said and followed Sims.

They walked along the wide-planked deck and Sims paused in front of a gleaming mahogany door with a brass sign, NUMBER ONE. The room inside was worthy of the finest hotel. It was paneled in dark rich wood with sparkling brass fittings. A big brass bed stood in the center and the wide bay windows showed a view of the broad river and the distant bank. The adjoining room held a large copper bathing tub.

"Dinner is served at six o'clock. Meanwhile, you just ring me if you want some hot water or anything else, sir," Sims said as he departed.

Fargo lay down on the wide bed and closed his eyes. Yeah, this was the life. A week of rest and good food, a hot bath every day, gambling, and some female company—he thought of the woman in red and wondered where she was staying. He felt the *Lady Luck* bobbing in the water, then heard the paddle wheel begin to churn. With a bump and a scrape the huge riverboat swung out into the current and gently rocked back and forth as it began its journey north and he let himself be lulled to sleep.

The gaming room was in full swing when he arrived later that evening. The rest, the hot bath, and the good meal served in his room had done him a world of good and he was ready for some entertainment. And as he stood looking over the riverboat's casino room on the main deck, he saw it was everything the advertisements had said it would be.

The wide room was hung with red velvet curtains and lit with golden gas globes that sparkled with prisms. At least a hundred people were crowded in, swarming the tables. Slick-haired gambling men with brooding eyes wore broadcloth coats, brocade vests, and diamond rings and stickpins. And these professionals stood shoulder to shoulder with wide-eyed country bumpkins clutching their chips, eager to win and destined to lose. The hurdy-girls in brightly colored satin dresses wove in and out of the crowd, clinging to the arms of the winners. Waiters in red velvet coats carried trays of champagne glasses. Blue-clothed faro tables and the green felt poker boards, keno, and chuck-a-luck tables were clattering with chips and cards and tokens. The roulette wheels spun and sputtered, while the cardsharps and conmen, the humbugged and the suckers, all threw down their money and took their chances.

A loud cheer went up from a table nearby and Fargo pushed his way forward. There a poker game was in progress and a solemn man in narrow blue spectacles was cleaning up. On the table in front of him was a huge stack of chips and cash and coins and, as Fargo watched, the dealer slapped down more cards and the man in the blue spectacles turned up four aces and raked in another armload of chips.

"How the hell does he do that?" a man standing nearby called out. "I bet he's got aces up his sleeve."

In answer, the gambler calmly rolled up his sleeves to expose his forearms and continued playing. Fargo grinned to himself. He knew exactly how the man in the blue spectacles was managing it. The deck was marked on the back with a kind of ink that could only be seen through blue glass. He'd seen the trick before.

Over the heads of the crowd, he spotted a familiar red ostrich feather. He had to push his way through to the table until he could spot Ruby Murphy sitting at one end. Her dark shining hair was piled on top of her head and fell in ringlets over her bare shoulders. Her red satin dress was edged in black lace and cut low to reveal the deep curves of her breasts. Diamond earrings glittered each time she shook her head. Of all the women on board, she was the most spectacular, her beauty like a dark and dangerous moon.

As he watched, her wide cornflower blue eyes glanced up from her cards and caught his gaze. Her heavy dark lashes blinked with surprise and for a brief instant, he saw the flicker of a smile on her lips, but she didn't acknowledge him and in the next instant seemed to gaze right through him and then turn her attention back to the dealer. A real game player, Fargo decided.

She was losing at twenty-one, and badly from the look of it, with only a short pile of chips in front of her and a couple of scrawled notes, as though she had already extended on the house.

"Hold," Ruby said softly, and several of the men standing around leaned forward eagerly—it was obvious the bunch of men were more interested in watching her than watching the game. Ruby came up eighteen against a pair of tens and pushed a few of the chips reluctantly across the table while biting her lower lip.

"Here, doll, take some of mine," said a silver-bearded man pushing some chips across the table toward her. Ruby flashed the man a grateful smile and blinked her eyes. Fargo turned away, deciding to find some other female company. Ruby Murphy was just too complicated, but as he scanned the room, he couldn't get the picture of her wide blue eyes and dark lashes out of his mind.

There seemed to be a lot of action at a nearby table and Fargo headed that way, deciding to join in. But when he got closer, he was surprised to see Josh Leatherberry gathering in an armload of coins at a game of faro. He was doing as well as Ruby Murphy had been doing badly.

Leatherberry's brown face was flushed with excitement and he raked his fingers through his ragged-cut brown hair as he peeked under the cards lying facedown in front of him. He tugged on his beard, then glanced over at the dealer and pursed his lips as if thinking hard.

In front of Leatherberry stood a virtual castle of chips, along with piles and piles of gold and silver coins in tall turrets. There had to be several thousand dollars there. The crowd around the table seemed to be holding its breath as Josh Leatherberry checked his cards again, then glanced heavenward and made a gesture like he was praying.

"Come on, Lady Luck, don't desert me now," Leatherberry whispered. He took no notice of anybody gathered around the table but instead, slowly, he slid a tall stack of coins toward the center of the table, then another and another. The dealer, his knuckles on top of the keno deck, was sweating nervously as he watched. Josh Leatherberry continued to move his stacks of coins.

"Why, he's going to bet it all, the dope." A dove in a yellow dress giggled.

Fargo smiled to himself as he realized just what Josh Leatherberry really was. To everybody else in the room, Leatherberry seemed to be a naive country fellow who had got a streak of good luck and was now getting carried away and was about to lose his shirt. But as Fargo watched Leatherberry's silk-smooth hands moving the chips and coins deftly across the felt, he knew he was watching one of the slickest gamblers he'd ever come across. Of course the man had smooth hands. Gamblers often sandpapered their fingers so they would be supersensitive to the small pinholes or scored edges of a marked deck. A good cardsharp would know what kind of hand he was holding with his eyes closed.

"Hold on now," the dealer said, loosening his collar and mopping his forehead. Leatherberry continued to push the stacks of coins and chips toward the center of the table. "You ain't going to let yourself go bust on one hand, are you? Don't you want to go home with something, fella?"

"You telling me you can't match my bet?" Leatherberry said, hesitating just a moment. "You telling me the big old *Lady Luck* doesn't have enough money to cover me?"

An angry buzz went around the table and one of the men standing nearby said it didn't sound fair to him.

"Of course not!" the dealer said, twisting his hands. "I just have to call the manager over, that's all. We . . . we have to see what we can do about, about this."

"About what? About me having a streak of good luck? Well, how do you like that?" Leatherberry said, rocking back in his chair and laughing. He caught Fargo's eye and grinned. "An old trapper from out West gets Lady Fortune to smile on him for once and the *Lady Luck* casino don't want to pay up if I win this hand!"

"That ain't fair," one of the onlookers shouted. "If a man's lucky, he oughta win."

But Fargo knew Josh Leatherberry was playing with more than luck. The commotion brought the casino manager on the run. He was a bald man with a green frock coat and one glance at the table told him all he needed to know. He glanced suspiciously at Josh Leatherberry, then glared at the dealer.

"I'm using a fresh deck of cards," the dealer protested, the sweat pouring down his face. His knuckles on the cards in front of him were white. "And this . . . gentleman wants to bet it all."

The manager's jaw tightened as his eyes shifted to Josh Leatherberry. Fargo could see what was passing through his mind. Usually the dealers and casino managers could spot the cardsharps well before things got out of hand. Usually they could cotton on to their ruses and get them evicted from the tables before they won too much money. But Leatherberry had seemed so much like a bumpkin that the dealer's suspicions had been lulled and, by whatever means Josh Leatherberry was cheating, he'd managed to stack up a good bank against the house. And now he was betting it all on a hand he was sure would win. And there was absolutely nothing the *Lady Luck* casino could do about it now without making the rest of the patrons angry.

"The house will cover your bet," the manager said in a tight voice and gave the signal for the dealer to show his hand. There was such a crowd that Fargo couldn't even see the faces on the cards, but the outcome was obvious. A shout went up from the onlookers and the dove in the yellow dress screeched and threw her arms around Leatherberry's neck, planting a big kiss on his lips.

"Table closed," the manager said. The crowd drifted away as did the dove when Leatherberry made it clear to her he wasn't buying. Leatherberry began gathering up his winnings. "I know your face now and I'm on to your game," the manager said as he handed over another bag of cash. "So don't show up in this casino again." The manager and the dealer stalked off.

"Nice work," Fargo said.

"Just lucky," Leatherberry said, hoisting the two bags over his shoulders.

"Yeah, like the kind of luck that brought you that Arabian?"

Leatherberry laughed in reply, his brown eyes twinkling.

Fargo decided to go check on the Ovaro and walked outside with Leatherberry, leaving the bright noisy casino behind. On deck, the Southern night air was warm and humid and smelled of honeysuckle. The hum of the engine and the slap of the paddle wheel on the water was soothing as the riverboat made its slow way up the wide muddy Mississippi. A full moon was just rising, its golden light glinting across the water.

Fargo gazed off to the west where the distant riverbank was thick with trees and humped by low mounds of levees protecting the cotton and sugarcane fields. Something caught his attention, not a sound, but a motion. His keen eyes searched the bank and he saw on the bank dim figures—men, maybe a dozen of them down in a thicket by the water's edge. They stood in a crowd on the bank while their horses were drinking from the river. As the moon rose and the light grew stronger, Fargo could see that they seemed to be looking out across the water directly at him, directly at the *Lady Luck* as it paddled up the river. As he watched, he saw the men mount and fall into formation, then ride in a dark line along the bank, weaving in and out of the trees but always moving upstream alongside the riverboat.

Fargo thought immediately of the men he'd overheard in the stable back in New Orleans. Could they be the same men who were looking for the woman in red they knew was traveling on the *Lady Luck*? Every instinct in him said Ruby Murphy was in deep trouble, despite her aggravating denial of it.

"Looks like a posse or something," Leatherberry said, breaking into Fargo's thoughts. "It's funny they look like they're following this boat."

"Yeah, my guess is that last casino you hit is going to catch up with you," Fargo said to allay the gambler's suspicions.

Josh Leatherberry laughed at this and they walked on to the stable, where the gambler hid his winnings among the hay and Fargo gave the Ovaro a long curry and said good night to Josh Leatherberry, who had bedded down on deck, continuing to play the part of the lucky country bumpkin.

Fargo decided to walk one more time around the deck but found himself thinking about the appearance of the riders onshore and wondering where Ruby Murphy was. Just then he heard voices ahead coming from the bow, speaking softly but hurriedly, anxiously. He stopped and crept forward silently until he stood a few yards away, hidden by a jutting corner. The wind carried the words toward him. He peered out and saw two figures standing at the bow. It was Ruby Murphy and the ship steward, Sims.

"Why yes, ma'am, I surely did get your letter," Sims was saying.

"And you were on board that night?"

"Oh yes, ma'am. Why, I've worked on the *Lady Luck* now for over forty years and I ain't never had a day off but Christmas."

"And you saw it happen?"

"I sure did, ma'am. I was standing near him as I am to you now. Right when he got shot and killed."

"Oh my God," Ruby Murphy said. She sounded like she was going to cry.

"Now, ma'am," Sims said. "It was a long time ago. Almost twenty years now."

What the hell was going on, Fargo wondered. He leaned closer, listening.

Ruby burst into sobs and Sims comforted her.

"You don't understand. All my life, I wanted to find out. The name," she said at last, sniffling. "Just tell me the name—"

Just then, a door banged opened behind him. Fargo whirled about. The dove in the yellow dress appeared, outlined in the light. She spotted him standing there and let out a delighted cry.

"Why, what are you doing up here all alone," handsome?" she said loudly. "Ain't you the one I saw with that lucky ruffian that gave me the brush-off? How's about buying a girl a drink?"

Fargo cursed to himself as he heard a clatter from around the corner, Ruby Murphy and Sims obviously starting in surprise. Whatever Ruby's secret was, he wouldn't overhear it now.

The dove in the yellow dress stood with one hand on her hip, impatient. "Well?" she said. "How's about it?"

A moment later, Ruby Murphy appeared around the corner, her blue eyes dark with suspicion as she glanced at him and flounced off down the deck. Sims followed, as if to pursue Ruby, but then someone called him from inside the casino. With a reluctant backward look toward the retreating figure of Ruby Murphy, the steward went inside the casino.

"Go hunting elsewhere," Fargo said to the dove as he turned to pursue Ruby. He caught up with her at the center of the boat, grabbed her arm, and turned her about.

"Let go of me!" Ruby said. "How dare you spy on me and listen to my private conversations!"

Fargo didn't even try to deny it. It was useless. Obviously, there was some secret here. She'd been trying to learn from Sims the name of someone who had shot a man years ago on the *Lady Luck*. Was her quest connected with the pack of men he'd overheard in the stables searching for a woman in red? If only she would trust him. Every instinct in him told him she was heading for danger.

"I just think that trouble's stalking you," he said. His eyes searched the wooded riverbank, but the riders he'd spotted earlier were not in sight. "Let me tell you what I saw tonight out there." And he told her what he'd seen and how he thought they might be the same men from New Orleans.

"A bunch of men looking for me?" Ruby Murphy said, tossing her head as if in disbelief. But in her tone Fargo heard the first dark note of doubt and of fear. There was something here that she was afraid of and her eyes followed his gaze across the glittering water toward the line of dark trees. But a moment later, she seemed to toss off her fears. She turned to look up at him, the moonlight falling across the lovely curve of her cheeks. "Why, the only man looking for me seems to be you," she said, blinking her long lashes and licking her lips with the tip of her tongue. Damn she was a flirt, he thought, and deserved what she was about to get.

He seized her in his arms and before she could protest, bent to kiss her, seeking her warm sweet mouth. She struggled for an instant, like a small bird in his grasp, then responded to him, her mouth opening to his searching tongue, a low moan in her throat as his hand sought the soft curve of her breast. He slipped his hand inside the neckline of her dress against the satin of her flesh, found the small hard berry of her nipple, and gently stroked it, and thought of taking it into his mouth. He could feel her breath quicken, the flutter of her heart.

"Oh," she whispered as he released her, then pulled her toward him and held her close. He could feel the hard throb of wanting to be inside her. She snuggled up to his chest and seemed to be trying to catch her breath as he stroked her silken hair. "Well," she said after a moment, pulling back and looking up at him. "You don't waste any time, do you?"

"Just giving you what you seemed to be asking for," he said with a smile. "Your room or mine?" Ruby stepped away from him and held on to the railing. She seemed embarrassed.

"Well, it seems I'm sleeping on deck," she said. She laughed then and tossed her head as if she didn't care. "You see, I busted the bank tonight. Lost everything I came with." She turned about and hoisted herself to sit balanced on the railing. Her dress inched up and he saw her small red leather boots and shapely calves in fishnet hose. She followed the direction of his gaze and swung her legs.

"There's plenty of room in my bed," he said, enjoying the view of her as she sat on the railing. With one hand, she played with a dark lock of hair that hung between her breasts.

He was just about to move toward her again when something thudded against the bow and the boat lurched. The engine whined and in an instant he realized they had run aground on a sandbar. Ruby cried out, her arms suddenly waving in the air, reaching and finding nothing as she fell backward. Fargo made a grab for her but his hand closed on air and he rushed to the railing just in time to see her disappear into the dark churning water. In a moment, he yelled out a warning as he stripped off his Colt and threw it down on deck.

The muddy roiling water was surprisingly cold as he dove cleanly into it, and came up, dashing the water from his eyes, looking around for her. Yards away he saw her thrashing, heard her sputtering and crying for help. And just beyond her, the huge paddle wheel was churning, thudding, as it headed straight for her. With his powerful arms, Fargo stroked through the water and felt the undertow of the powerful wheel, the water tugging on him. Ruby Murphy suddenly disappeared beneath the waves with a scream just as he felt the current begin to drag him under.

2

The powerful undertow of the water seized him like dark hands, pulling him beneath the water. The thudding of the mammoth paddle wheel vibrated through him as Fargo fought the pull of the undertow, and struck out with his strong arms straining against the whirling current. He kicked upward, came to the surface for a moment, gasped for air, and saw the blades of the wheel slicing through the water. Where the hell was Ruby? She was nowhere in sight. She must have gone under, was about to be cut up by the beating of the mighty-engined paddleboat. He dove then, straight into the whirling water, fighting hard against the pull of the paddle wheel, reaching in all directions for a long tortured minute, his breath burning in him, almost losing hope as he felt himself swept nearer to the throbbing wheel, until in an instant his fingers brushed something in the murky water—something. He swam toward it, grasped a handful of fabric, her dress, pulled hard, felt her come toward him. She was limp and he grasped her round the waist. The beating of the motor and the wheel was like the heartbeat of a gigantic beast, his lungs bursting, the cutting blades inches away as he dove deeper, forcing them down deeper into the blackness of the water as he felt the sucking paddle wheel pass just over their heads. The throbbing began to diminish and holding her body close to his, he shot upward toward the surface of the river.

The air burned his mouth, his hungry lungs. He bobbed in the rippling wake of the riverboat, gasping a few deep breaths. Then he pulled Ruby's head above water, shook her. She remained unconscious, her body slack. He paddled in the water, shook her again. The paddleboat was steaming upriver but he heard the yells of men on deck. They'd been spotted and the boat would come around and rescue them. But the bulky craft was slow-moving and would made a wide circle before coming about. It would be a good ten minutes before they were picked up. For Ruby, it might be too late.

A moment later, he saw something dark looming above the water. A log or tree branch of some kind. Fargo swam toward it, felt something beneath his feet, and found himself waist-deep on a sandbar, where a tree had floated by and caught. He pulled Ruby up and threw her over the tree, head down, and slapped her on the back. Just how much water had she taken in? At first she didn't respond and he began to despair. He pressed against her back again and in a moment, she recoiled, sputtered. He hit her again and heard the water come, her coughing, gagging, as her lungs cleared. She coughed again and again, until she was breathing free. All the while, he held her on the log, her slender waist between his hands. Then the coughing turned to sobbing and she turned to him as he gathered her into his arms. Despite the warmth of the hot summer night, her skin seemed cold as snow and she was trembling. Fargo stripped off his wet jacket and wrapped it around her, for all the good it would do. He held her against him as he watched the riverboat's golden lights chugging toward them.

"Oh my God," Ruby said. "I thought I was going to die." She sounded like a little girl.

"You almost did," he said, tightening his arms around her. He rubbed her skin, trying to give her some warmth. She shivered beneath his touch.

"How can I thank you?"

He bent to kiss her again, her cold lips warming slowly to his, pressing her quivering body against his broad chest. She shuddered again.

"You'll need a hot bath when we get back on board," he said. The sound of the riverboat came nearer at an angle. He glanced up to see that there was a crowd on deck leaning out over the railing trying to spot them in the darkness. He called out and waved and someone saw him. The riverboat corrected its course, came about, and a small rowboat was put over the side. In another few minutes, they were being lifted over the railing of the *Lady Luck*.

"That was some trick, Trailsman," Josh Leatherberry said, stepping out of the crowd and slapping him on the back. "I saw that lady go under and I thought she was mincemeat for sure. I never saw anybody go through a paddle wheel and come out the other end in one piece."

"Give the folks some room now," Sims said loudly over the hubbub of the passengers. He stepped up and shooed the crowd back, then brought a woolen blanket which he wrapped around Ruby Murphy. By twos and threes, the gawkers melted away back into the casino.

"Miz Murphy, you can't exactly be sleeping out in the night air after such a fright," Sims said worriedly. "You'd be needing a hot bath to get you right again."

Ruby seemed suddenly shy.

"She'll stay with me," Fargo said, putting his arm around her. "So we'll be wanting some hot water drawn."

"Sure, Mr. Fargo," Sims said, turning away, his eyebrows raised. Josh Leatherberry said good night with a wink and headed off toward the stables. Fargo walked her around the deck to the door of his suite.

"It's lovely," she said, looking around at the rich dark wood and the large brass bed. Sims appeared in a few minutes and began filling the large copper tub with pails of hot water. Even though it was unnecessary, Sims drew the curtains across the huge bay windows that gave a wide view of the river above the copper tub.

Ruby sat on a chair and all her self-confidence seemed to have disappeared. She held the blanket wrapped around her. Her damp hair curling around her head made her look younger somehow. She gazed down at the carpet as Sims went back and forth with the hot water until the tub was filled, then brought in Ruby's red leather luggage. Fargo gave Sims a gold eagle and with a wide grateful smile the steward departed.

Ruby Murphy sat in silence, not looking up. Fargo walked over to the mahogany cabinet, took out a cut crystal decanter, and poured two glasses of brandy. The amber liquor sparkled in the golden light of the oil lamps.

"This will make you feel better," he said, handing it to her. She didn't look up at him but sipped it. A moment later, she rose and went into the bathing chamber. He noticed she only closed the door halfway. He stripped off his sodden clothes and donned a silk robe he found hanging in the closet. He stretched out on the bed sipping the brandy and listening to the light splashing sounds of Ruby in the copper tub.

"Fargo?" she called out softly, tentatively.

He rose and went to the door and opened it slowly.

"Skye," he said. She smiled as she lay back in the gleaming tub, her pale arms stretched above her head, her dark hair a halo around her beautiful face. Her white breasts tipped by rose-colored nipples and large aureoles were wet and gleaming.

"Skye," she repeated, almost in a whisper. "Wash my back?"

He picked up a sponge from the washstand, approached, saw through the clear still water her narrow rib cage, swelling hips, the curves of her legs, the dark tangle of fur. He bent to kiss her and held her head as her hands came up behind his neck, caressing him, playing with his ears as his tongue sought hers. He dropped the sponge, slid his hand down the front of her to brush across the slippery curves of her breasts, lightly pinching her nipples, which crinkled in his touch. Her mouth drank him in, pulled his tongue deeper into her, hungrily. He slid his hand down into the water, down the arch of her belly to find the wiry triangle, the exquisite folded lips. She shook as he touched her there. He felt her breath quicken as his fingers sought her deeper, entering her, opening her, the gloss of her tunnel slick and hot. His cock was engorged, aching to be inside her. Suddenly he stripped off the robe, pulled her upward and she came to her feet, like a sea creature dripping and glittering in golden lamplight, her finely shaped body a delight of curves.

"I want to thank you—"

He put his hand to her lips.

"Not like this," he said. "Wanting is the only reason."

He kissed her again, held her small wet frame against him, felt the warmth and coolness of her flesh against his, the subtle thrust of her hips as his cock pressed at the threshold of her. He stroked her breast and kissed her eyelids as she shuddered uncontrollably.

"Oh yes, Skye. Yes, I want you. Please."

He lifted her in his arms and carried her to the

bed, then stretched out beside her. She pulled his hand between her legs, and he found the hard seed of her fruit, gently rubbed it and felt it swell, her lips wet and engorged with desire. He flicked his tongue against her breasts and kissed her neck as she moaned. Her hips moved under his hand and he felt her tightening.

"Skye, yes, there. Oh, I'm coming, yes . . ."

She shuddered and he knelt between her legs and pulled her hips upward, the tip of him entering her wet doorway, pushing upward into the welcoming warmth of her tight around him. She cried out, clinging to him as she came, shivering and quaking, and he plunged into her, his cock swelling to fill her, thrusting again and again, shallow and then deep as she cried out and met each of his thrusts with her own. He held her breasts in his large hands, pushing into her softness. Her legs came up around him and he entered her more deeply, heard her moan.

"Oh, oh, I'm . . . yes, yes, again—"

And he felt her orgasm overwhelm her again as he let himself go, let himself shoot up inside her as they came together, plunging as if into a whirlpool of desire, of oblivion, of forgetfulness, as their bodies met and gave, and he gave himself to her, everything, until at last he was spent.

Later, she lay nestled in the crook of his arm, sleeping peacefully. The boat was rocking as it steamed northward. He watched the moonlight wash over the lovely curve of her hip. She looked so innocent, so vulnerable, as she slept. But he knew better, knew that there was some secret here. For a while, he thought about the dark riders he had seen on the riverbank and wondered how and whether they were connected to the woman he held in his arms. Who was Ruby Murphy really? Then he let sleep take him too.

Fargo woke at dawn, slid out of bed, and washed up with a pitcher of cool water, then dressed. He suddenly noticed it was quiet and that he missed the sound of the riverboat's engine. The boat had obviously docked during the night and now pitched gently to and fro in the Mississippi current.

Ruby stirred, lifted her head, and blinked her cornflower eyes, surprised for a moment. Then she rolled over and rested back against the pillows, half covered by the sheet. She smiled contentedly and stretched her arms overhead. He enjoyed the sight of her generous breasts.

"More?" she said with a smile.

"Oh yes. After breakfast," he proposed.

"Ummmm," Ruby purred. "Yes, I'm hungry. Very hungry."

"I'm going to check on my pinto. I'll get Sims to bring us breakfast here in the suite."

"That would be fine. And I think I'll have another bath," Ruby said. She got out of bed and he admired her naked form as she tiptoed across the room.

"*Another* bath?" he teased, pinching her. She shrieked, then giggled and paused in the doorway and looked in at the copper tub. The sunlight from the huge bay windows fell across the room.

"Oh, yes," she said. "I didn't get to finish my bath last night. I got interrupted."

He kissed her, enjoying the new familiarity of her mouth, the way her breasts fit his palm. She let him go reluctantly and as he left she was opening the bay windows above the copper tub to let in the morning light and breeze.

When he emerged on deck, he saw that the riverboat was moored to a huge old disintegrating dock that was as overgrown as a jungle. Thick moss-bearded tree branches hung down almost to the water, obscuring the shore. Few people were up and about.

After he ordered breakfast from Sims, Fargo spent the next hour seeing to the Ovaro, giving it a good curry. The horse was restless, cooped up in an on board stable. It longed to be galloping out in the open country. For a moment, Fargo considered taking it for a run but there was no telling how long the *Lady Luck* was going to be moored to the bank. When he emerged from the stable, he ran into Josh Leatherberry.

"Some strangers came on board," Leatherberry said, jerking his thumb over his shoulder.

Fargo saw what he was pointing at. Back at the stern, a couple of men in range clothing stood talking to several of the passengers. The two men, their faces weatherworn and their hands rough, were from out West for sure. They looked like the ranching type. Fargo wondered what had brought them aboard and he sidled over to investigate. One of the passengers, a rotund talkative lady with wispy white hair, was babbling on about the casino and who had won what. She spotted Fargo approaching.

"And, why, this is the very man who jumped in the water and saved that lady, just like I was telling you," she said to the two strangers as she peered at Fargo. "Hey you, young man," she called out. "I've found out everything about you but I don't believe I even know your name. Why, my name's Myrna Floyd, Mrs. Floyd that is."

As she spoke, the two strangers slipped away in the other direction as if they had heard enough of the old woman's talk, but as they were walking across the deck, Fargo saw them glance back at him. There was something about their looks he didn't like, something that spelled trouble.

"Who were they?" he asked the old woman. Josh Leatherberry came up to listen.

"Oh, you're the hero of the ship," said Mrs. Floyd, ignoring his question. "Why, the way you jumped into the water last night and saved that lovely girl in the red dress—"

"What were you talking to those two men about?" Fargo asked her sharply. Mrs. Floyd pursed her lips at his tone. The two men had disappeared from sight on the other side of the ship.

"You think they might be—?" Leatherberry left the rest of the question unspoken.

"Why, we were just talking about this and that,"

Mrs. Floyd said peevishly. "I don't see it's any of your business."

"What you were talking about might not have been any of *your* business," he retorted. "What were they asking you? Be quick about it."

"Oh, just who was on board. Who was staying in what rooms," she answered, startled. "You know, that kind of thing." Fargo had heard all he needed to hear. He turned away from the old woman and began striding across the deck in the direction in which the men had disappeared, with Josh Leatherberry following. But they had hardly got ten yards when his worst fears were confirmed. He heard a woman's scream, then the sound of gunfire. He swore and broke into a run, heading for the sound of the commotion, which came from the direction of his suite. The door was locked and his key did not open it. Several passengers, drawn by the furor, gathered around. Inside Fargo heard the sounds of movement, scraping and bumping.

"What the hell's that?" Josh Leatherberry asked.

Fargo called out to Ruby and got no answer. He swore, drew his Colt, and shot off the lock. Still the door held shut. It had been blocked inside by something like a heavy piece of furniture. He heaved against it, once, twice, again and again until it burst open. Inside, the room was disheveled. The door to the bathing chamber stood ajar. He threw it open with his Colt in hand. The room was empty.

A glance told him what had happened. The bay windows stood wide open and he ran to them. Just outside, a few feet below the window, was the rickety board dock. Low flung branches scraped against the boat. He peered into the green shadows of dense undergrowth. He leaned out and heard the whinny of horses in the near distance.

"Goddamn it," he cursed. It was clear what had happened. And he had missed them by just moments. Behind them, some of the passengers looked into the broken door.

"You think it was the same men we saw the other night?" Leatherberry said. "I thought it looked like they were following this riverboat. They must have been trying to get Miss Ruby."

"Damn right," Fargo said. "I'm going after her." He grabbed his gear and pushed through the muttering crowd, heading back to the deck.

"Hey, you mind if I come along?" Josh Leatherberry said as he followed him to the stable. Fargo stopped and looked at him in surprise.

"What's your interest in this?" He spoke sharply, hastily. Every minute counted now. Every minute that bunch of men were getting further away with Ruby Murphy.

"Well," Leatherberry said, "I'm not exactly welcome at this casino. I could use a little adventure. And I'm just curious to find out what this is all about."

"So am I," Fargo answered. "You any good with a gun?"

"In my business, I gotta be," Leatherberry said, pulling a small silver derringer from his pocket. A deadly weapon in the right hands, albeit only at close range.

"Sure, come along," Fargo said. "I could use the help."

They ran toward the stables and got their two horses saddled and their gear loaded on. Fargo found one of the ship's crew and ordered the gang-plank put down to the dock. The crew moved so infuriatingly slowly that he and Leatherberry had to practically do the job by themselves. All the while, Fargo kept an eye out for Sims and even asked one of the crew members to fetch the old steward, but he couldn't be located and word came back he was off duty and was probably napping somewhere.

Fargo cursed to himself, wishing there was time to locate the old man and to find out what it was that Ruby Murphy had been trying to find out. Maybe it was that piece of information that had got her into trouble. But when the gangplank was nearly in place, they still couldn't find Sims and Fargo realized a good half hour had passed since Ruby had been taken. He couldn't delay any longer.

"Let's go!" he called out to Josh Leatherberry as the wide-planked gangway was made secure onto the old dock beside the *Lady Luck*. They led their two horses down off the boat and into the thick branches that overhung the old dock. Fargo looked for a path and found a dark tunnel through the un-derbrush. Leading the Ovaro by the bridle, he plunged into it. After a few yards, he turned around and looked back toward the river but the casino riverboat was already out of sight, hidden by the thick foliage.

"This is like some kind of hell," Josh Leatherberry said, as his boots sank into the swampy muck and he pushed through the mossy thickets.

Fargo was too busy tracking to answer him. The marks were clear in front of him, the path where the two men had left their boot marks. In a few minutes, they reached higher ground where the underbrush gave way to dense trees. There Fargo saw signs that three horses had been tethered there. He and Josh mounted and rode slowly through the dappled woods as he followed the horses' hoof marks cut deep in the moist earth. They rode at only a walk and Fargo could feel the pinto's eagerness to be galloping out on the open trail again.

The terrain could not have been worse, swampy land choked with underbrush. The mosquitoes whined around their heads like a black cloud and the branches were thick and almost impenetrable. They were just lucky the trail was so clear, Fargo thought. They had gone only half a mile when he found another clearing with even more tracks.

"Looks like they met up with the rest of that gang here," Leatherberry said, looking down at the confusion of marks in the wet clay. "How many you think there are?"

"Looks like about twenty," Fargo said. There was nothing more he could read from the tracks in the clearing and they rode on. All day, and the next and the next, for long seemingly endless hours they fought through the steamy bayous and quagmires of Louisiana. Each night, they found a mound of dry land and made a campfire, eating and resting for a few hours only, then pressing on, through the groves of live oaks, sassafras, and sweetgum, plunging back into the sludge and slog of the cypress swamps.

For the most part, the men they were following kept to the higher ground, the mounds of dry earth that wound through the muck and occasional lakes. But here and there they had to ford streams and rivers, or plunge chest deep into bogs and reedy marshes. The gang didn't seem to be bothering to hide their tracks, but seemed more concerned with speed.

On the fourth day, Fargo sat on the Ovaro, looking down at the fresh tracks that marked the dirt trail leading along the wooded edge of a silent lake. The sun was just rising and the mist still hid the water. A loon called hauntingly. The tracks had led west, angling north just slightly toward Texas as they gradually climbed to higher land and now they were nearly to the border. They had almost caught up with the gang, were only minutes behind them. The sound of a horse's whinny reached their ears.

"We'll dog them all day," Fargo said. "We'll have to stay back far enough so they don't catch sight of us. Once night falls, we'll go in."

It was an easy day's ride now, and the land grew slightly rolling and dry, easy on the horses. There was no need for speed today and if anything, they needed to drop back a bit in order to avoid being spotted. As they let the horses walk along, Fargo kept a sharp eye out ahead. Meanwhile, he suddenly was overcome with curiosity about Josh Leatherberry.

During the days of traveling together, Fargo had gained an appreciation and a liking for the wiry man. Despite his smooth hands and his life as a professional gambler, Josh Leatherberry was clearly a man used to the open country and had a degree of trail-craft that made him an easy traveling companion. Now he wondered what the man's story was.

"How'd you get into the gambling business anyhow?" Fargo asked as their two horses walked side by side up an easy road.

"Why, I've been a gambler since I was tall as a stack of poker chips." Leatherberry laughed. "When I was just a tyke, I used to organize poker games in the schoolyard. When I got older, I took to the road, got myself some fancy duds with my first earnings. Only I found out wearing a diamond stickpin and flashing rings gets the casino owners suspicious faster than an extra ace pinned to your chest."

"So you started dressing like a bumpkin," Fargo said. "Almost fooled me when I met you."

"Almost?"

"Your hands are too smooth for a trapper," Fargo said. Josh Leatherberry held up his hands and looked at them ruefully. "And then there's your horse."

Leatherberry grinned and patted the neck of his Arabian.

"Yeah, my pride and joy," he said. "I got lucky on this horse. But usually my take's not too much. I try to keep it to around ten percent. That way, the house doesn't have cause to kick me out and they don't bar me for being a professional."

"You didn't do that on the *Lady Luck*."

"Well," Leatherberry replied, "I knew that boat would get a little claustrophobic and I decided to blow it all in one night. And if they threw me out, what the hell?" He patted his saddlebag. "Made a good two thousand dollars. That will keep me going for a while."

By nightfall, Fargo reckoned they had crossed the border into east Texas. A few farms lay scattered here and there and the lowlands were dotted with lakes and sumps. The sun was a huge orange ball sinking slowly into the gray moist air. All day, Fargo had been careful to keep back from the gang they were following so the men did not catch sight of them. Now, as darkness gathered beneath the stands of sumacs and the post oaks, it was time to make their move. They slowed their horses to a quiet walk and, eyes and ears alert, made their way up the road. Finally, at the top of a short rise, Fargo lifted his hand and they halted. There in front of them, across a ragged field and at the edge of a dark wood, was the golden wink of a campfire and the black figures of men and horses. They could hear the distant sound of a harmonica playing and a few men singing off key.

There was no need for words. They dismounted, hid the horses in a thicket, and crept forward, taking cover in the thick serviceberry bushes that dotted the field. As they came nearer, Fargo could make out the details of the camp. Some of the men were fixing dinner—the smell of roast meat and onions made his mouth water. Others were tending the horses and, Fargo noted, taking good care of them. Others sat by the fire singing or talking. They seemed well disciplined but, as he watched, there didn't seem to be anyone in charge. In the center of camp was a single canvas tent and he guessed he would find Ruby Murphy there. He hoped the men had not mistreated her.

He and Leatherberry were crouching behind a stand of serviceberry. They weren't keeping too good a watch, he noted. It would be an easy matter to get in closer. He whispered his intention to Leatherberry, who held a silver chased pistol in hand and nodded silently, indicating he would stay put and cover Fargo in case of trouble.

The waning moon was rising when Fargo slipped out of the brush and, crouching low, made his way by short dashes closer to the camp. At last he took cover, lying flat on the ground behind a large log at the edge of the camp. From this position, he could overhear everything the men were saying. At first, all he heard was idle chatter. Several of the men were clearly talking about their wives and the fact that they were family men surprised him. Then the conversation shifted to ranching matters and they talked about a bad infestation of cattle mange and how best to treat it. They didn't sound like a gang of kidnappers or desperados, Fargo thought to himself. Dinner was served up and then the men all sat down to eat. Fargo peered over the log and saw one of the men with a plate of food and a tin mug go to the tent.

"Miss Murphy," the man said tentatively.

"What do you want?" It was Ruby Murphy's voice, Fargo noted with surprise, but it had a rough note of impatience in it.

"Would you be wanting some supper?" the man asked.

In answer, Fargo saw the tent flap open slightly and Ruby's hand came out, took the food, and disappeared again. The man returned to the campfire and all the men were silent for a long moment.

"Maybe we ought never to have done this," one of the men said quietly. Fargo strained his ears to hear.

"Yeah, we could get us in big trouble if we get caught."

There was another long silence as all the men ate. Finally, one man threw his plate aside in anger.

"Well, I say what the hell choice did we have? He's got us over the barrel and he ain't played straight."

"Now, Al, we don't know that for sure."

"Well, I know it for sure," the one called Al said. "I know I been had and I'm not going to go down without a fight. And if the law ain't going to help, then hell, we gotta help ourselves."

The men muttered assent at this and finished up

their dinner. And although he sat listening for the next hour as the men prepared to bed down for the night, he never learned anything more.

An hour later, as the moon rose higher, Fargo sat up and looked over at the campsite. The fire was a red ember glow. The mounds of sleeping men lay here and there across the ground. Several of them were snoring loudly. The one man who was supposed to be on guard had sat down on a rock near the warm fire and now he was slumped forward, asleep. A barn owl gave its wheezy cry from the nearby woods. It was time.

Silently as a shadow, Fargo rose and picked his way through the sleeping forms toward the white canvas tent. A breeze stirred and the door of the tent fluttered. A man mumbled and rolled over. Fargo froze as the sleeping guard sputtered, then quieted again. Three steps from the tent, then two, then one. He knelt and entered, his eyes adjusting to the dimness inside. She was lying asleep in a nest of blankets, her dark hair strewn about her.

Ruby Murphy awakened in an instant. And seeing the dark form of a man standing above her, she sat up with a jerk. He could see it coming and he made a lunge for her, tried to get his hand over her mouth before it happened.

But he was too late. Ruby Murphy let out an earsplitting scream and outside, the camp of men came awake with shouts of alarm.

3

Ruby Murphy's scream resounded throughout the camp of sleeping men and in an instant they were awake and sounding the alarm. There wasn't a second to lose. Fargo cursed under his breath as he grasped her arms. She struggled, still not recognizing him in the darkness of the tent.

"It's me—Fargo!" he said in her ear. In an instant she was still. "No time to explain."

Someone was approaching. There was no place to hide. Just then a shot rang out in the distance, then another and another. It came from beyond the perimeter of camp. It was Josh Leatherberry trying to divert the men's attention. In an instant, Fargo had a plan. He pushed Ruby toward the tent flap.

"Tell them you saw a man in your tent and he ran away. That's why you screamed. Quick!"

Before the approaching man had a chance to look inside, Ruby did as she was told. Meanwhile, the gang outside was shouting to one another, confused and uncertain.

"Who was that? He keeps shooting! He's getting away!" one of them said.

"So let him!"

"He might be a spy. We've gotta catch him!" Fargo started with recognition. The last man who had spoken had a gravelly voice, low and unmistakable. He remembered it from the voices he'd overheard at the stables back in New Orleans.

Outside, Josh Leatherberry continued to fire an occasional shot. This seemed to convince the men they'd have to give chase. Fargo heard the sounds of horses being saddled. This was just the time when they would be the most distracted.

"Let's go!" he said to Ruby.

"Now? But—" She clutched a blanket to her. "I'm not dressed." He noticed she was wearing only some flimsy lace undergarments that clung to her curves. She took a moment to pull on the red leather skirt and blouse that she'd carried in a bundle, along with stockings and boots.

As she dressed and gathered the rest of her things into a bundle, Fargo pulled the Arkansas toothpick from its ankle scabbard and slit open the back of the tent, then peered outside. All was clear. The men's attention was successfully diverted as they got their horses ready.

He grasped Ruby's arm and pulled her out the back. Hunching low to the ground they ran toward a nearby stand of chokecherry, then huddled there for a moment. Fargo looked back at the campsite, where all was chaos and furor. They had managed to slip away without being seen. At least for now.

It took another ten minutes to make it back to the spot where the Ovaro was hidden in a thicket.

Once, they had to duck into the bushes as the men on horseback careened by. Josh Leatherberry seemed to be keeping the gang chasing off in the other direction, away from Fargo's hidden pinto. When they reached it, Fargo stowed her bundle in his saddlebag, then pulled her up onto the saddle to sit in front of him. He put his arms around her, enjoying the soft warmth of her roundness against him.

By now, the sound of pursuit was fading into the distance. Leatherberry had done a damn good job of helping them get out of camp, Fargo thought gratefully. The wiry gambler was a quick thinker, a good trail companion. The only problem was that he and Leatherberry hadn't made any plans for a place to rendezvous in the event they were separated. Nevertheless, he was sure once Leatherberry shook that gang off his tail, he'd look for Fargo's tracks and turn up again. Meanwhile, they needed to get some distance between themselves and the few men left back at the camp who were bound to look in the tent eventually, find Ruby missing, and then coming looking for her. That could happen any moment.

The pinto burst out of the thicket and headed up the road, galloping hard and full out under the dim light of the half moon. Fargo let it have free rein and gave the distant camp wide berth. In an hour, they were miles away and galloping through open land with low hills. Well after midnight, he reined in beside a brook bounded by deep cutbanks. He dismounted, then lifted Ruby down from the horse and led the pinto to the water.

It was just as good a place as any to spend the rest of the night, he thought, looking over the spot. Here in the trough between the cutbanks, their camp wouldn't be visible to anybody riding by on the trail unless they practically stumbled in on top of them. He unsaddled the pinto, pulled a blanket from the saddlebag, and found a sandy spot against one of the banks. Ruby snuggled up next to him and he wrapped the blanket around them against the cold night air. The stars winked overhead.

She was warm and soft in his arms, her breasts like pillows. He slipped his hand beneath her blouse and found the nipple, brushed it lightly until it hardened beneath his fingers. She purred in her throat and he kissed her, his tongue exploring her mouth, his hands on her breasts, then trailing up her bare leg to find the warmth between her legs, the tickle of fur, the wetness as he stroked her, felt the tight button contract as she came and her back arched as her hips moved under his touch. Her hand moved up his thigh to find his hardness beneath his jeans. She fumbled with the buttons until she put her hand inside to grasp his hard cock in her cool hand. She lay back and he knelt between her legs, pushed up inside her wet warmth as her legs came up around him, welcoming him into her familiarity.

"Oh yes," she said, moving under him as he pumped into her tight sheath and she cried out as she came again and he gave himself to her, the surge of his coming, deep into her, again and again, waves of light and darkness beneath the turning stars. After a while they lay back and listened to the coyotes serenade in the distance.

"I'm sorry I screamed back in the tent," Ruby said as she nestled against him. "You surprised me. I never expected you to come rescue me." He kissed her lightly, noticing her voice had turned to honey again. "That was the second time you've saved my life. Thank you, Skye—again."

"Oh, I don't think those men were going to kill you," Fargo said. "But why did they snatch you?"

"I have no idea!" Ruby said. There was something in her tone that told him it was a bald-faced lie. "I've never seen any of those men in my life. Honest."

"And you have no idea in the world why they might be interested in one Ruby Murphy?" She must have heard the brusqueness in his voice.

"Really, Skye," she said in her breathiest voice. "I'd tell you if I knew anything. Honest I would." He wanted to believe her. But he knew she was lying. Well, never mind.

"So, where to now?" he asked her. "Do you want me to take you back to New Orleans?"

She shook her head and seemed to think for a moment.

"I guess I'd better get to Blackgulch," she said. Then she brightened. "Yes, Blackgulch. Why, my brother Mort has a big business there and he's got a lot of money. If you take me to Blackgulch, I'm sure he'd give you a reward. For saving me as well as for bringing me there."

Blackgulch. There it was again. That one decipherable word on the garbled telegram that had tried for three months to reach him. Was it the same Blackgulch? His instinct told him that there was trouble there in the town and that the answer would turn out to be yes.

"Just where is Blackgulch?" he asked nonchalantly.

"Here in Texas," Ruby said, "just north of Fort Worth."

"A couple days' ride from here. Nice cattle country up there," Fargo said thoughtfully. It was some of the richest grazing land in the country and full of longhorns. Ranchers were just starting to see the potential in the country thereabouts since they could drive the cattle across the Indian Territory to the north and up to Kansas City to meet the rail lines for shipment to the markets back East. "Is your brother a rancher or what?"

"Oh, no." Ruby laughed. "Mort runs a gambling casino."

"If he's got a lot of money, isn't it likely those men were going to hold you for a ransom?"

"Definitely not," Ruby snapped, her voice suddenly harsh. Then she caught herself. "I don't think so, Skye," she said sweetly. "I don't think any of those gentlemen knew I was even related to Mort. In fact, I don't think any of them even know who Mort is. I'm sure they don't. No, they were just—just—"

She shrugged and left the sentence unfinished. The moonlight sculpted the curve of her cheek and glittered in her eyelashes, and by her silence Fargo knew he'd hit right on it. The men had kidnapped Ruby because of something to do with her brother. And she was protecting him. But what was the connection?

Yes, she was lying. But eventually, he'd find the truth.

Sleep came uneasily and his dreams were filled with men holding hands of cards that couldn't be read. At dawn, he left her curled in the blanket and went to the stream, where he washed up in the cold clear water and refilled the canteens. He stood in thought as the pale sun slipped upward into the burnt apricot clouds and the larks were reveling loudly in the brush. Swifts darted across the sky. It would be a clear day, a good day for travel.

In a few minutes, he had made a small almost smokeless fire of dry grasses and twigs, just large enough to boil water for a pot of coffee. The smell of the brew woke Ruby and she rose, stretched, and then folded up the blanket and joined him. They breakfasted on dried berries, nuts, and some hardtack biscuits, which turned edible only when you dipped them in hot coffee.

He had just packed up the supplies and was ready to ride on when in the distance he spotted a rising dust cloud. Was it the gang in pursuit? He cautioned Ruby to remain hidden behind the cutbank as he gazed across the plain. His keen eyes picked out a lone rider and after a few more moments he recognized the long lean gait of a fine horse, an Arabian. Indeed, it was Josh Leatherberry.

Fargo didn't risk a shot, since it was impossible to know if any of the gang were still in the vicinity and might come to investigate the sound of gunfire. Instead he waited until Leatherberry drew closer and then he climbed up from the cutbanks and hallooed and waved. Leatherberry spotted him at once and galloped in their direction.

"A friend of yours?" Ruby Murphy said with a slightly distasteful tone as Leatherberry came closer and she could see the man's rustic clothes and rough-cut hair.

"It it weren't for Leatherberry, you and I would never have got out of that tent back there," Fargo said to her.

"I think I saw him on the *Lady Luck*," Ruby said.

"That's right, you did," Josh Leatherberry said, overhearing her words as he reined in and dismounted. He introduced himself and stuck out his hand. Ruby declined to take it, but nodded.

"You're the gambler who won a lot of money on the *Lady Luck*, Mr. Leatherberry," Ruby said. "How did you do it?"

"Do it? Hell, I wish I knew! That ways I could do it again! I had the best, most luckiest night I ever did have," Leatherberry said enthusiastically, slapping his thigh. He was playing the part of the naive country bumpkin again, Fargo saw. "So, we gave those ruffians the slip, did we? Where to now, Fargo? Are we taking Miss Murphy back to the riverboat or what?"

"She wants to go to Blackgulch, Texas," Fargo said.

"Oooooo—eeeee!" Josh Leatherberry said. "Blackgulch, Texas! Why, ain't that the even *more* luckiest break I ever did have? There's supposed to be gambling right in Blackgulch. And I got so much money now and I'm on such a roll, I think I'm going to try my luck again."

"Ruby's brother owns a casino in Blackgulch," Fargo put in.

"*The* casino in Blackgulch," Ruby said proudly.

"You don't say," Leatherberry said. Fargo caught something subtle in the gambler's tone, a hesitation, a dark note, but a moment later it was gone and the enthusiasm returned. "Why, the Blackgulch Gaming House is s'posed to be the best in the West!"

Ruby dimpled at the compliment to her brother's establishment. She looked beautiful in the morning light, Fargo thought, the red leather skirt outlining the roundness of her hips and her slender waist. Her wide eyes were as pale blue as the dawn sky and her hair shone like black fire. But somehow the more he got to know Ruby Murphy, the less interested he became in her. There was just too much she was hiding from him. And even though his instinct told him she was lying to protect her brother, somehow he didn't trust her motives. There were two kinds of people, Fargo thought. With some, you knew right away what they were really made of, could see right into them. And with others, they just got more and more complicated—and the complexities usually weren't to the good. He was beginning to suspect Ruby Murphy was one of those kind.

"Let's get going," he said.

The two days passed quickly and they made good time galloping across the wide plains of eastern and central Texas. The land grew drier, the lakes and marshes giving way to rich grasslands like a rippling ocean in all directions clear to the circular horizon. The Ovaro easily carried him and Ruby both, but they loaded the supplies onto Josh Leatherberry's Arabian. Mile after mile, the land changed. There were fewer trees and patches of gray sage appeared. Between the gently rolling hills ran narrow rivers edged with tall cottonwoods.

This was ranchland of the highest quality, Fargo thought as they rode along. And the men who were building up their herds now, amassing lands in this region, might one day be rich—or perhaps their children would be. At the moment, a man had a lot of hard tasks to face in raising cattle here. First of all there were rustlers. And then it was hard to get good ranchhands to help. And there was the problem of having no way to fence such vast regions of grassland, so a rancher had to depend on his brand to identify his property. To keep his herd together, a rancher set up a system of line-riders, cowpokes to ride the perimeter of the ranch continually to keep the herd from straying too far off the land. And then there was the weather—some years there came blizzards so bad, the stock froze standing upright. And other years brought droughts so bad, the water holes became mud and then cracked earth, and the cattle died of thirst.

And for all that work, with a little luck, a man could turn a good profit if, in the end, he could get his cattle up to the railroad lines in Kansas. The big hope, however, lay in the future—someday the railroad would come to Texas. It wouldn't happen soon. Some folks said it wouldn't happen in their lifetimes. But when it did, the ranchland of north Texas would be as valuable as gold.

By the evening of the second day, they were five miles from Blackgulch. The sun had set and the dark gathered like water on the wide plain while the sky still held the light, and rosy clouds floated above where the sun had set. The evening star appeared.

They cantered down the wide track at an easy pace. Blackgulch lay just ahead. The trail rose over a slope and then descended toward a shallow gully and a long line of cottonwood trees, black in the gathering dusk. They let the two horses break into a fast gallop as the gravity of the downhill run pulled them along. They had just entered the grove when Fargo smelled trouble. They were not alone. The pinto whinnied, having smelled something too. Fargo cursed himself for not having been more alert, for having let himself be lulled by the easy approach to the town, but the Ovaro was hurtling forward and it was too late to turn back.

In the next instant, he spotted the dark figures of

horsed men massed beneath the trees and he drew his Colt, cursing silently.

"Oh, shit," he heard Josh Leatherberry say.

Ruby hadn't spotted the men yet, but when she did, she gasped and pressed herself against his chest, turning to hide her face in his arm.

Just their luck, they had run smack into the gang, he thought as he spotted a dozen, two dozen, maybe more, dark riders waiting in the shadows of the cottonwoods. The riders brought their horses about immediately. They were surrounded.

"Hold up there," a whining voice called out. "We gottcha covered now."

For a moment, Fargo considered shooting their way out. But then he realized how badly they were outnumbered. Now he could see maybe forty men in the grove, all on horseback, most of them with pistols in hand. They didn't have a prayer of escaping. Leatherberry glanced at him and after exchanging a silent look, Fargo slowly raised his hands away from his holster. Leatherberry followed suit.

"That's better. Who the hell are you anyway?" the whining voice said again. Fargo spotted a heavy-set fellow riding up. "Who are you?" the man repeated his question. "And why are you riding into Blackgulch after dark?"

"I can ride where I like. It's a free country, isn't it?" Fargo retorted. Outnumbered or not, he didn't like the man's voice one bit. He acted as if he owned the town. Just then the faint starlight above caught the glitter of a five-pointed star on his chest and he relaxed a little.

"You the sheriff of Blackgulch?" Fargo asked.

"Yeah," the man snapped. "Good guess. Now who are you?"

"Why, you're Lars Hulbert!" Ruby broke in. "My brother Mort Murphy has written me all about you."

"Your brother—why, you're Mr. Mort Murphy's sister?" the sheriff asked. Fargo heard the sudden deference in Sheriff Hulbert's voice. "Well hell, why didn't you say that in the first place? Why, Mr. Murphy is the number one citizen of Blackgulch. He told me you was coming to town, Miss Murphy, but he wasn't expecting you until next week." Sheriff Lars Hulbert had suddenly become talkative and downright obsequious. "Why, me and the boys will be happy to escort you into town."

"That's very nice of you," Ruby Murphy said grandly.

They fell into a column and Sheriff Hulbert rode beside Fargo's pinto, talking to Ruby and ignoring him entirely. Which was just as well, Fargo thought as he listened and tried to take the measure of things. As they rode toward town, Fargo turned about for a moment in his saddle and looked back at Josh Leatherberry who rode behind him. Then he noticed that every man in the column seemed to be wearing a tin star on his chest.

"You got more deputies than I've ever seen in one town," Fargo said when the sheriff and Ruby had a pause in their conversation. "You got trouble in Blackgulch? Cattle rustlers maybe?"

"Yep," the sheriff said smoothly. "Rustlers are our number one problem. We got a helluva time with cattle rustlers, don't we, boys?" he called out. A few of the men muttered assent. "But it's a damn peaceable town thanks to me and my boys and we aim to keep it that way." Fargo heard the implied threat in the sheriff's words. Then Sheriff Hulbert fell back to talk to a few of the men riding at the back of the column.

"So, all you fellows must be ranchers from hereabouts?" Fargo asked, directing his question to one of the men who rode beside him, a huge bruiser of a fellow with close-cropped hair on his square skull and a neck and arms thick as oaks.

The huge fellow looked over at Fargo with narrowed eyes, as if considering whether to answer the question or not.

"I ain't a rancher," the huge man said thickly. "The name's Bo Boggs. I'm a full-time deputy. And I'm from Missouri. I ain't from around here."

"Really?" Fargo asked. "Is that true of all these men?" The big fellow nodded and Fargo was surprised. That was unusual in the West. Usually when a sheriff needed help, he just deputized a few of the more upstanding citizens and everybody pitched in to keep the peace. Hiring men from outside as deputies was usually far too expensive for a small town in the West. The whole setup was strange, Fargo thought.

There were a few lights ahead and soon they

were riding down the dusty main street of Blackgulch. It wasn't much to see, especially at night. A few ramshackle false-fronted buildings defined the main commercial street. There was the usual Emporium, its darkened windows crowded with dry goods including everything from yards of calico, to coils of jute rope, to barrels of salted soda crackers. The sheriff's office stood adjacent to the undertaker's, and the stables were across the street next to a small rundown hotel. There was a row of sod houses too, a few lamps glowing in the windows here and there. But what made Blackgulch different from the hundreds of other tiny towns that dotted the West was the Blackgulch Gaming House & Casino, a huge board building that stood just at the far edge of town.

Rising higher than anything else, Mort Murphy's casino had been built of weathered boards cut into fantastical gingerbread shapes and then painted in garish colors—orange and pink and yellow and bright blue—worthy of a circus. The batwing doors swung open from time to time as men came and went and the noisy laughter and shouting from inside echoed through the dark and quiet streets of the town. The whole exterior edifice was lit with flickering gas lamps and topped by a huge sign which read: BLACKGULCH GAMING HOUSE & CASINO. GOOD CLEAN FUN, CHECK YOUR GUNS AT THE DOOR, NO DOVES ALLOWED.

Fargo was surprised. Usually, the casinos ran a bordello operation on the side, along with a flourishing trade in liquor. But he was beginning to suspect that nothing in Blackgulch would be as he expected.

"There it is," Ruby said. "Mort's dream come true."

Sheriff Lars Hulbert was riding alongside them again.

"You oughta be real proud of your brother, Miss Murphy," the sheriff said. "Why, before Mort Murphy came to Blackgulch, this town was practically dying. And now, thanks to him, we got the casino just like in the big city. And Mort Murphy made it all possible."

"You get a lot of gambling men coming through town?" Fargo asked.

"Not really," the sheriff answered. "We don't like strangers. We got a peaceful town and strangers bring trouble. The casino caters to the local men."

They came to a halt and tethered the horses. Ruby slid down from the Ovaro, took her bundle from Fargo's saddlebag, and eager to see her brother, hurried inside.

Fargo and Leatherberry followed through the creaking batwing doors. A young man stepped forward to check their pistols. No one in the casino was allowed to carry a weapon except for the sheriff and his men, Fargo noted. And they all seemed to be carrying small weapons, derringers maybe. The huge room was filled with dozens of tables covered with green or blue felt. There were roulette wheels, faro, chuck-a-luck, keno, and poker, and twenty-one games in progress. The clatter of chips and coins and dice filled the air, punctuating the background noise of cheers of the winners and groans from the losers.

Suddenly, a tall man came forward through the crowd and because of his commanding presence Fargo examined him closely. He was thick in the chest, his black hair slicked back, with gray along the temples. Bushy black brows accentuated gleaming obsidian eyes that seemed to miss nothing. He was a fancy dresser, dapper and all in white, a golden watch chain crossing his ivory brocade vest and diamond rings sparkling on the thick fingers of both hands.

"Ruby!" he boomed. Mort Murphy—Fargo didn't need to be told it was he—sighted his sister and picked her up, hugging her. He was as large and bearlike as she was petite and yet when Fargo saw them together, he could see the family resemblance in their dark eyes and their expressions.

"And this is the man who saved me—twice!" Ruby said, motioning Fargo to come closer. "His name is Skye Fargo."

Mort's expression changed instantly, his dark eyes growing even darker even while he kept the wide smile on his face. Fargo felt Mort's gaze examining him.

"Skye Fargo? *The* Skye Fargo? The one they call the Trailsman?"

Fargo nodded and Ruby Murphy looked at him curiously.

"Is he famous or something?" she asked her brother.

"One of the most famous men in the West," Mort

Murphy said. Ruby looked at him with greater interest while Fargo was trying to read Mort's expression. "So, what brings you to Blackgulch?" The casino owner seemed tense, wary.

"Just delivering your sister," Fargo said lightly. "Then I'll be heading on out."

Mort Murphy seemed to relax at this answer.

"Well then, let me give you a little token of my appreciation. Five hundred dollars worth of chips! On the house."

"Thanks," Fargo said, keeping his private thoughts off his face. A real reward would have been hard cold cash, not casino chips that could tempt a man to play them—and chances were good, lose them back to the house. And for a man like Mort Murphy, five hundred dollars was not exactly generous. Not for saving his sister's life. Not that he really needed the money or expected it. But the gesture told him a lot about what Mort Murphy was made of. "And this is the other man who saved your sister," Fargo said, gesturing to Josh Leatherberry and introducing him. Mort's eyes passed glancingly over the rustic figure.

"Well, the two of you can share the chips," Mort said, not at all interested in Josh Leatherberry. Mort waved his hand grandly about. "Have a wonderful time—on the house! And now, my dear sister," he said, taking Ruby's arm, "you must be exhausted. And we have so much to talk about—the little matter of—" Fargo saw Ruby's face darken and Mort promptly stopped and glanced around.

The two of them moved off into the hubbub of

the gambling crowd, their heads close together. They were too far away for Fargo to hear their words, but he saw Mort Murphy ask his sister a question. She shook her head no and whispered something into his ear, something that obviously made him angry. Murphy stamped his foot, his dark brows lowered, his face red with rage. After a moment, he recovered, nodded, as if in resignation, then took Ruby's arm and moved off. Fargo wondered if it had anything to do with the name Ruby Murphy had been trying to get out of Sims, the steward on the *Lady Luck*. Unless he was mistaken, she hadn't managed to talk to Sims again before she had been kidnapped. Fargo looked around and noticed that Lars Hulbert and his men had taken up stations around the casino, as if they were keeping the peace. Fargo and Leatherberry stood looking over the action.

"There's not one professional in the bunch," Leatherberry said, shaking his head as he surveyed the crowd. "Every one of these players is a local."

Fargo could see what Leatherberry was talking about. At most casinos, there was at least one table of high rollers, professional gambling men who were drawn by the action and had come for high stakes. But here, there were only ranchers and cowpokes in their dust-stained clothing. These locals hung over the tables excitedly, tossing down chips and peeling cash from their back pockets to buy more when they lost.

There wasn't a woman in sight and when the men ran out of chips, some waiters came by with drinks on trays and pockets full of more chips the men could buy.

"You want to play?" Fargo asked.

"Not tonight." Leatherberry shook his head. "Let's go find the local flophouse."

They left the casino and led their horses back down the dark street to the stable where they made arrangements for their mounts to be well taken care of. Then they took their gear to the nearby hotel. In the lobby, a dead palm tree in a brass spittoon stood beside a worn-out horsehair couch. The grandfather clock was stopped at eight o'clock. Behind the battered oak counter, an elderly man slumped in his chair, snoozing.

Fargo rang the bell, but the man continued to snore. After several more attempts, he reached over and shook him. The old man proved hard of hearing and they had to shout to get two rooms booked for the night.

The rooms weren't fancy but were clean. Fargo washed up and was about to turn in when he realized he had stowed some of his gear in Leatherberry's saddlebags earlier that morning to accommodate Ruby Murphy's bundle. He knocked on the gambler's door and entered to find Josh Leatherberry sitting on the bed, surrounded by a collection of his gambling apparatus, along with numerous decks of cards.

"Ah ha!" Fargo said. "All your gambling trade secrets."

Leatherberry looked rueful.

"What *is* all this stuff?" Fargo asked. He picked

up a strange metal armature with thin rods and a kind of spring clamp attached.

"Oh, that's called a holdout," Leatherberry explained. "Fits under the table or up your sleeve. The card attaches here." He demonstrated by clamping an ace into the apparatus and then deftly retrieving it between two fingers. "It's called that because you can hold out a card from a game until you need it. And this is for marking cards," he explained, showing Fargo a delicately engraved brass box with an arm and delicate needle attached that would pierce a card with subtle pinholes that could be felt by the gambler who knew they were there. Another device shaved cards along the very side and a practiced cardsharp could tell the suit and number by the convex or concave curve of the edge.

"Amazing," Fargo said.

"Of course, if you're really good, you don't even need them marked," Leatherberry said. He picked up a deck of cards, fanned them out to show they were in random order, then began to flutter them like a flock of birds taking flight, his fingers moving with lightning speed as the cards flew through the air in a steady waterfall, again and again. And after a few minutes of this fancy shuffling, Leatherberry dealt out the cards from the top of the deck . . . four aces in a row, then the kings, the queens, the jacks. Fargo laughed. He'd seen a lot of men handy with cards, but he'd never seen one quite as good as Josh Leatherberry.

"I'm looking forward to seeing you in action," Fargo said. "Must be quite a show."

"If I do it right, it's no show at all. In fact, you don't even know it's happening. It ought to just look like I keep getting dealt some lucky hands."

Fargo laughed again, retrieved his gear, and returned to his room for a good night's sleep.

After breakfast, Fargo left Josh Leatherberry still working on his gambling equipment and decided to have a look around the town. He stepped out of the hotel onto the boardwalk and looked around. The dusty street was fairly empty at this hour in the morning, the browns and grays of the weathered board storefronts and the few sod houses in marked contrast to the garish bright colors of the Blackgulch Gaming House that rose at the far end of the street.

A familiar figure pushed through the batwing doors of the casino. Mort Murphy, with his black hair slicked back and silvered at the temples, spotted Fargo and waved. He hurried across the dusty street. Today he wore a pale blue suit of expensive cut that was perfectly tailored to his broad chest, and gold rings glittered on both hands. He looked completely out of place in the small rough town of Blackgulch.

"Fargo!" he called out. As he came up, he grasped Fargo's hand as if they were old friends. "I didn't see you last night at the tables. Did you lose all your chips early and go home?"

"No," Fargo answered shortly. He didn't like

Mort Murphy's instant familiarity. It seemed false and shallow. The abrupt answer brought the casino owner up short and his black eyes examined Fargo's face.

"How long do you plan to stay in Blackgulch?" Murphy asked. The shift in his tone of voice was subtle, but unmistakable. He was damned eager for Fargo to get out of town.

"I plan to cash in my half of the chips and get," Fargo said, adopting a lighter tone to lull any suspicions Mort Murphy might have. "Although it seems to be a nice place."

"Oh yes," Murphy said, the relief evident in the sudden relaxation of his broad shoulders. He gestured grandly down the street. "Blackgulch is a fine town, upstanding town, fine people."

They walked along the boardwalk in the morning sun while Mort Murphy talked about how he'd looked all over the West to find just the right place to put a gambling casino and how Blackgulch had proved to have the perfect location. As he listened, Fargo kept his poker face on while the thoughts swirled in his head. Blackgulch was a terrible location for a gambling house. It was a small town full of ranchers barely making a living. There wasn't a major trail nearby to bring in travelers, unless you counted the cattle trails heading northward to Kansas. And the sheriff had said the casino was mostly for the locals, not for any strangers passing through. As he listened to Murphy, Fargo wondered why he was bothering to make such a point of why Blackgulch was such a perfect location, when it was plain it just wasn't.

They were passing the Emporium when an older rotund woman with flaming red hair and a faded calico dress, her arms full of packages, burst out of the door and bumped smack into Mort Murphy. He caught her as she tottered off balance. Her paper-wrapped packages flew everywhere.

"My gracious!" she exclaimed as she regained her footing.

"Good morning, Mrs. Dottie Hawkins," Mort Murphy said. He took the woman's hand and grandly kissed it, then bent down and began to collect the packages that had fallen all over the boardwalk. Fargo helped. Murphy straightened up and grandly handed the stack of packages back to her.

"Here you are, my dear lady," Murphy said. "Isn't that a becoming color on you. Why, I think all the ladies back East are wearing just that shade of green this year. I always know you're wearing the latest fashion."

Mrs. Hawkins blushed at his deference and blinked her eyes as she held the packages in her red-roughened hands. Fargo thought Mort Murphy was overdoing the gallant bit. She suddenly seemed to notice Fargo standing there and Mort Murphy introduced them.

"Mrs. Hawkins is married to one of the most important ranchers in these parts," Murphy explained. "Al Hawkins is a fine man. One of the upstanding pillars of this community." Mort Murphy was sure laying it on thick. Dottie Hawkins blushed again at the compliment to her husband.

"Community," she said, repeating his word. "That reminds me!" She knelt and put the packages down a moment, then straightened up and fished around in the net reticule at her waistband. From it she pulled a small piece of creased paper and a pencil. "The Fourth of July is coming up soon. Now have you gentlemen made your contributions to the First Annual Blackgulch Patriots Celebration? The ladies committee has big plans but we need some money—"

Fargo handed over a five-dollar gold eagle, which delighted Mrs. Hawkins.

"How would this be?" Mort Murphy said, pulling out his wallet and removing a hundred dollars. Fargo was mildly surprised at Murphy's generosity.

"Oh, Mr. Murphy!" Dottie Hawkins gasped. "Why, that will take care of everything. Thank you!" She tucked the money into her bag and grew thoughtful. "You know, times have been hard this year. Nobody seems to have any extra money to spend. Every rancher we know seems hard up this year. And Al says . . ." She left the sentence unfinished. Fargo saw the lines of worry that scored her forehead suddenly deepen. For a moment, he became aware she seemed to be carrying a great burden.

"Oh, that's just because the annual cattle drives haven't gone north yet," Mort Murphy said encouragingly. "Everybody is going to make plenty of money this year. Now, don't you worry. Besides, your husband won big at my tables last night."

"He *did*?"

"Sure, he's one smart man, Al is," Mort said. "Why, if there were more ranchers around like him, my whole casino would go bust!"

"He never tells me anything," Dottie Hawkins said.

"Oh, he's probably waiting till some moment he's going to surprise you," Murphy said hastily. He grandly picked up the packages and returned them to Dottie Hawkins' arms. "Now don't you go telling your husband that I let you know about him winning. That will be our little secret."

"Oh, of course!" Dottie said. She started moving off, muttering under her breath. "Well, my birthday is coming up in two weeks . . . maybe Al is going to tell me then—"

Mort Murphy bid Fargo good-bye and entered the Emporium.

As Fargo turned to watch Mrs. Hawkins depart, he noticed the slender figure of a young woman leaning against the tethering post. She had ridden up on a gleaming ebony horse and dismounted while the three of them were talking, and now he realized she had overheard their conversation, in fact had been standing there listening in. The young woman's honey blond hair fell in a smooth cascade over her shoulders. She wore a man's plaid shirt and jeans which emphasized the grace of her long legs and narrow hips. Her brown eyes were focused on Mrs. Hawkins as she passed by in the street, still muttering.

"Dottie, you're being a fool," the young woman suddenly said. The older one came up short. "Don't you trust anything that two-bit cheat says."

"Betsy Cahill, you mind your own business," Dottie Hawkins said in a huff. "You're just jealous because until Mr. Murphy arrived, your pa practically ran this town. And now that Mort Murphy is so popular with everybody, your pa is mad. You and he don't like the competition."

"That ain't it and you know it!" Betsy Cahill said, her face flushed. She stamped her foot, seized the bridle of the horse, and stomped off, disappearing down an alleyway. Fargo stood in thought as he watched Dottie Hawkins climb into a rickety wagon and drive away down the street. He wondered about Betsy Cahill, who obviously didn't trust Murphy. Well, neither did he. And suddenly, he wanted to ask her about that.

He followed the direction she had gone, walking down a narrow alley between two board buildings until he came to a ramshackle barn. Outside, Betsy's ebony horse stood tethered. Inside, through the open double doors he glimpsed hay and stalls. He heard the sounds of movement inside and he walked to the door, peering into the gloom. In a moment, his eyes adjusted to the darkness. There on a pile of hay, he saw the form of Betsy Cahill, her honeyed hair strewn around her, her eyes closed. Her shirt was unbuttoned and gaped to reveal her small breasts tipped with dark nipples. Between her long legs, a huge man was kneeling, struggling to pull the jeans down off her hips. Betsy Cahill was out cold.

Silently, Fargo drew the Colt from his holster and pointed it at the skull of the man who was about to rape her.

"Get off her," Fargo said. The huge man froze at the sound of his voice, then slowly turned about, an angry sneer on his face. It was Bo Boggs, who started as he recognized Fargo's face.

"This is none of your business," Bo Boggs said.

"I'm making it my business. Now get up." His finger tightened on the trigger.

A slow sinister smile spread across Bo Boggs' face, the tiny eyes in his slack face glittered.

"Maybe you want a piece of this for yourself?" he asked.

"I'm warning you," Fargo said, impatient.

"Sure, I'm willin' to give you some."

Fargo had had enough, but an instant later, he realized Bo Boggs had been stringing him along, buying for time. Because in that instant, he saw the eyes of Boggs shift for just the flicker of a second to something, someone, standing right behind him. And in that instant too, he heard the small crackle of dirt beneath the sole of a boot and a heavy blow smashed hard against the back of his head, hard enough to bring whirling stars and a rushing noise in his ears as he saw the straw-strewn floor of the stable coming up. The spinning world began to go black.

4

The dim stable whirled and darkness closed in on all sides as the pain from the blow radiated through his skull. He felt his body falling through space, knew he was losing consciousness. The stable floor came flying toward him, hit hard, and he felt his body roll over as if from a far distance, heard a man laugh, and the rage welled up in him, red and hot. The pale square of the open stable doors wavered before his eyes as if he were underwater. He swam through the darkness, fury pounding in his blood, holding on to the square of light, forcing himself. He felt his fists clench, the fingernails digging into his palm, the pain of that bringing him to clarity, fighting the enormous throb in his head.

"He's out cold," a voice said. "Let's do her."

Someone, a dark figure, leaned over him and he felt a hand fumbling for his Colt, trying to remove his fingers from his gun, and then the rage welled up again, a gigantic wave that opened his eyes and he pulled the barrel up in an instant, hard against the man's grasp, willed his mind to pull the trigger.

The Colt exploded, the gunfire rupturing the waves in his head. The dark figure looming over him staggered backward at the force of the bullet, then sank to his knees and fell forward. He twitched once, twice, and then lay still. A spurt of bright blood ran from the dark hole in the man's chest and a rivulet snaked across the dirt floor, soaking into the earth.

"What the hell?" Bo Boggs screamed.

Fargo rolled over on the floor, the Colt held steady now, his vision clear as anger. The huge man kneeling in the hay was terrified, his small eyes white all the way around. He suddenly looked around in a panic, spotted his pistol lying on the floor a few feet away, and made a lunge for it. But Fargo pulled the trigger again and the gun went spinning across the stable floor, out of Bo Boggs' reach.

Fargo got to his knees, tried to keep them from shaking. The Colt was trembling a little and he held his arm close in to his side to steady it.

He ought to just shoot the bastard dead, he thought as he glanced for an instant at the woman's half-naked figure lying on the hay. It looked as if Bo Boggs hadn't managed to get her pants off her before Fargo came around again. At least there was that. There was some rope hanging on the wall. So he'd tie the bastard up and wait until Betsy Cahill came around again.

"Down on your hands and knees," Fargo ordered. Bo Boggs squinted at him and Fargo waved with the barrel until the big man complied, dropping down to kneel among the hay and dirt.

Hell, his head hurt. He backed up slowly, keeping Bo Boggs covered every second. At every step, his knees threatened to buckle and the stable spun. He gritted his teeth. He had to keep hold on himself. He stepped over the dead man on the floor and his hand reached out and found the length of rope. Then he came forward slowly.

"Chin on the floor," he ordered Boggs. "Hands behind you." The huge man hesitated, then he felt the barrel of the Colt pressed into his back. "I mean business. I won't hesitate to put a hole in you if you try anything sudden."

Boggs did as he was told. With one hand, Fargo deftly pulled one end of the rope around the man's arms, while continuing to hold the barrel against Boggs' back. He brought one foot up and stepped on the rope as he knotted it with one hand. For a moment, he considered putting the gun aside to use both hands but he realized he was too weak to counter Boggs, even with his hands tied, should he pull something. His Colt was his only advantage. Bo Boggs' hands were tied tight enough to hold for the moment.

He was about to straighten up and tell Boggs to roll over so he could tie his legs when Betsy Cahill groaned. For a bare instant, he was distracted as he saw her suddenly stir on the hay. In that instant, Bo Boggs made his move, suddenly lashing out, kicking with one leg and catching Fargo's booted foot, throwing him off balance, his throbbing head still spinning.

He kept a grip on the Colt as he hit the ground and Bo Boggs struggled to his feet. Fargo rolled to one side, the gun pointed upward at Boggs. The huge man took one look at Fargo and ducked as the pistol exploded. Then, his hands still tied behind his back, Boggs spun about and ducked out of the stable door.

Hell, the bastard was getting away. Fargo leapt to his feet, his head whirling, and ran after him, pausing at the door to see Boggs running down the alleyway. Fargo squeezed off a shot, saw Boggs pitch sideways and stagger with a yelp of pain before he disappeared around the corner. Well, he'd got him in the thigh, but the bastard was still running. But in a small town like Blackgulch, there wouldn't be anyplace for him to hide. On the other hand, he might return with some of his friends.

Fargo walked over to the dead man and turned him face up. The jowly face looked vaguely familiar, maybe from the casino, and he was wearing a tin deputy star just like Boggs. If this was the kind of deputy Blackgulch was hiring, there was no question the town was in trouble. Fargo wondered if Sheriff Lars Hulbert knew what kind of men he had in his posse. Well, he would soon. There was no time to lose.

But before that, he'd have to take care of Betsy Cahill, get her someplace safe. And then he'd go after Boggs.

He walked over to the pile of hay. Her shirt was

open, her rounded breasts with their dark nipples and aureoles were small and beautifully shaped. He lifted her head gently, but she was still out cold. He felt the desire in him, but pushed it aside as he buttoned up her shirt. Her tight jeans had been pulled down over her hips and he saw the top of her golden fur between her legs. He knelt down and struggled to pull them up. At the motion, Betsy Cahill stirred and her eyes started to flutter open.

Suddenly a shot exploded beside his head, missing his skull by a fraction of an inch.

Goddam it! He pitched sideways, away from Betsy Cahill in case the bastard tried another shot. He rolled in the hay, fumbling for his holstered Colt, his head pounding again, cursing himself for not being more attentive. Clearly, Bo Boggs had got his hands loose and come back for revenge.

"Get your hands in the air, stranger!" a man yelled, his voice quivering with rage. The voice was not Bo Boggs'.

Fargo came out of the roll and leapt to his feet, Colt in hand, facing down a stocky gray-haired man who appeared in the stable door. The man's ruddy weathered face and thick shoulders marked him as a rancher for sure, as did his wool jacket and the long rifle in his hand.

Fargo stared down the round barrel of the rifle. He held the Colt before him. It was a standoff.

Over in the hay, Fargo heard Betsy Cahill coming back to consciousness. She groaned and he heard a movement as she sat up. He did not dare glance over at her, but kept his eyes locked on the stocky man who stood in the doorway.

"You all right, Betsy?" the man called out. "I got this man in my sights and I'm about to plug him dead."

"Pa!" Betsy cried out with a sob. Fargo heard her get to her feet and run across the floor. She came into his view, buttoning up her pants. After a moment, Betsy turned about and glanced at Fargo, her face white with fear. Then she looked at the dead man on the floor.

"It wasn't either one of these, Pa," Betsy said. "It was Bo Boggs. He hit me from behind and probably thinks I didn't recognize him, but I saw his face before I blacked out." The man's rifle wavered as he took her in one arm as she clung to him, sobbing with relief.

"That's right," Fargo said. "I surprised Boggs in here and that dead man there must have been his pal. He gave me an egg on the back of the head. But I ran Boggs off. Just for your information, I was trying to get your daughter back *into* her clothes before she came to."

"It did kinda look like that," the rancher said, "but I wasn't pausing to find out."

The implications of what Fargo had said suddenly dawned on Betsy Cahill and she blushed, hid her face in her hands and refused to look in his direction.

"And as to Bo Boggs," Fargo continued, "I plan to follow him, round him up, and take him to Sheriff Hulbert."

"Lot of good that will do." The rancher laughed scoffingly. "Bo Boggs is one of Hulbert's men. They can damn well do what they please to the likes of us. Obviously you ain't from around here." He lowered his rifle. "Guess I misjudged you entirely, stranger. The name's Paul Cahill and this is my daughter, Betsy."

Fargo smiled in her direction but she still didn't look at him, clearly embarrassed at the fact that she realized he had seen her naked.

"Skye Fargo," he said.

At the sound of his name, Betsy glanced up curiously, despite herself and Paul Cahill grinned widely.

"The one they call Trailsman?"

Fargo nodded.

"Well, I'll be damned," Cahill said. "Always wanted to meet you. We hear lots of stories about you. Why, you been all over the West. And here you are plunked down in this two-bit town of Blackgulch. What brings you here?"

Fargo considered the question for an instant, wondered how much he ought to say and decided he'd find out more about the Cahills before taking them into his confidence completely. He liked the look of them—they seemed the honest and hard-working kind. But still, he wanted to find out more. He answered lightly, "Just passing through. Not staying long."

He noticed that Paul Cahill's green eyes sharpened, suddenly full of questions. The rancher had heard the momentary pause before he answered, knew he was keeping something back.

"Well, I want to thank you, Fargo, for saving my girl here." He tightened his arm around Betsy Cahill, who glanced shyly at Fargo from time to time. "But by tangling with Bo Boggs, you made yourself a real enemy."

"You can't mean to tell me you're going to just let Boggs get away with this," Fargo said hotly.

"What can we do?" Paul Cahill shrugged. "Bo Boggs is one of Lars Hulbert's men and what Lars says goes."

"What Mort Murphy says goes," Betsy put in.

"I gather from what you said to Mrs. Hawkins, you don't think much of Murphy," Fargo said.

"Why, that cheat's got this whole town wrapped around his finger." Betsy exploded, her brown eyes aflame. "The only holdouts are Pa and me. This used to be a nice quiet community until that casino moved in. And now every rancher in the county is ruining himself in there every night. It's shameful. All except Pa."

"I guess I'm the only man over twelve who doesn't gamble in this town," Paul Cahill said, stroking his chin. "This wouldn't have happened to anybody else's daughter. That's because they're all in Mort Murphy's pocket. But not me—oh, never mind all that. I'll just have to keep a closer watch on Betsy from here on out."

"That's not good enough," Fargo said. "I'll get a U.S. marshall or one of the circuit judges in here.

There must be a way to bring that bastard to justice."

"Forget it," Paul Cahill said tiredly. "Mort Murphy and Lars Hulbert have got this town sewed up tight. What they say goes. And do you think in court my Betsy would be believed? It's hopeless." Paul Cahill, his arm around his daughter, turned away, then glanced down at the corpse on the floor. "And that dead man is going to get you in some trouble. Watch your back, Fargo."

"Come out to the Flying C sometime," Betsy said, looking back at him. "We're northeast about ten miles, over by Sawtooth Creek."

"You'd be welcome, Fargo," Paul Cahill said. The two left the stable and led Betsy's red out toward the street. Fargo stood in thought, angry at the injustice that allowed a brute like Bo Boggs to almost ruin a young woman and get away with it. Paul Cahill didn't seem like the helpless kind, and yet he was clearly so beaten down by the situation, he'd just given up.

Fargo walked down the alleyway and walked along the boardwalk. The door to the sheriff's office stood open. Now was as bad a time as any. He walked in.

Lars Hulbert sat at his desk, chair tipped almost backward, his beaklike nose pointed up to the ceiling, his big belly like a mountain, his eyes closed. A barber in a striped shirt leaned over him, brushing soap suds on his swollen face, then stropping his razor. Lars opened one eye, spotted Fargo, then shut it again.

"You put a bullet in my deputy," Sheriff Hulbert said in his high quavery voice. "And I heard you killed another. I could arrest you and string you up for that, Fargo. If I wanted to."

"Your deputy was about to rape one of the rancher's daughters," Fargo said hotly. The barber moved forward tentatively and razored off a long strip of suds and whiskers, then another.

"Oh, that little Cahill girl is a floozie," Hulbert scoffed, waving off the barber. "Why, she's been wiggling her ass at Bo Boggs ever since he arrived. From what I hear, he was just giving what was coming to her."

It was hopeless, Fargo thought. When the sheriff in a small town was corrupt, the whole place went rotten. And that's exactly what had happened in Blackgulch. The barber was almost done, was trying to negotiate his razor through the folds of the sheriff's neck, which was as wattled as a chicken's.

"Ouch!" Hulbert shouted. He slapped the barber's hand away and grabbed for a towel. Blood stained the white cloth from the nick on Hulbert's neck. "Now, look what you done!" he shouted at the barber, who was hastily packing up his things. The barber fled and the sheriff sat up, rubbed his face with a towel and peered at Fargo with his pale watery eyes.

"Let me give you some advice, Trailsman," Hulbert said. "Keep your nose out of the local romances. It ain't none of your business. And as to shooting my deputy, well I'm a reasonable man. I guess Mr. Murphy is obliged to you for rescuing

Miss Murphy. So, I'll give you two days to stick around Blackgulch. After that, if I see you around, I'll have you arrested. Got that?"

"Sure," Fargo said. He turned about and left, the rage boiling in him. All along the boardwalk, the citizens of Blackgulch were strolling or shopping or hurrying about their business. As he passed the Emporium, a mountain wagon pulled to a halt in front and the driver called out a delivery for Dottie Hawkins. The Emporium owner, a short balding fellow, came out the front door wiping his hands on his apron.

"Got a delivery here for a Mrs. Dottie Hawkins," the driver said, consulting a piece of paper. "Says to deliver twenty boxes of ammunition to her care at the Emporium."

Fargo almost whistled. Twenty boxes of ammunition? What would Dottie Hawkins be wanting with that? There must be some kind of serious trouble brewing if she was ordering that kind of ammunition supply.

"Oh, the bullets," the bald man said, stroking his pate. "That's for the Patriots Day celebration. You can stack them just inside my door. I'll keep them for Mrs. Hawkins." The driver pulled the canvas off the back of the wagon and Fargo saw cases of bullets stacked inside.

"What's the idea?" Fargo asked the bald man as the driver carried the crates one by one inside the Emporium. "You planning to have a shoot-out on the Fourth of July?"

"Nah. It's Mrs. Hawkins' idea. She wanted to

have a hundred-gun salute, only she wanted it safelike. You know, no stray bullets killing somebody's pet cat. So, she ordered all these boxes of blank bullets. Everybody's supposed to use blanks on the Fourth of July. That woman thinks of everything," he added with a shake of his head as Fargo moved off down the street.

The sun was well past noon and he was hungry. He found Josh Leatherberry practicing some new card deal up in his hotel room and the two of them walked out to find some grub. Several passersby told them the best lunch deal was at the Blackgulch Gaming House, so they headed for the tawdry-colored building. Fargo was surprised to find that the casino was crowded even in early afternoon. About half the men there were eating at tables and the other half were gambling at the tables.

At the door, they were stopped by one of Lars Hulbert's men, a young fellow with a shock of unruly brown hair and a tin star, who checked their guns and stowed them in a locked wooden bureau. Fargo noticed that all the deputies in the joint were carrying small silver carved derringers, all alike.

"Check out those matching guns," Leatherberry said with a twinkle of amusement in his eye.

"Mr. Murphy insists," the brown-haired deputy said importantly. He held the small derringer in the palm of his hand and gave them a look at it. It was a good weapon for the close quarters of a crowded casino. A man could palm it and swing it around easily and it was accurate enough at close range. Then the deputy showed them a glass case where all the rest of the derringers were stored. "See, we check our regular guns just like everybody else."

"Why is that?" Leatherberry asked.

"Oh, Mr. Murphy thinks it looks nicer if we carry these smaller guns rather than our rifles and pistols. More genteel-like."

"Genteel," Leatherberry said with a smirk. They turned away and went to find a table. A waiter brought them two tall roast beef sandwiches with horseradish along with mugs of beer. The food was good, Fargo had to admit. Leatherberry didn't say much but seemed to be looking around at everything very carefully. Fargo was struck by how similar and yet how different the Blackgulch Casino was from any other he'd ever seen. The gaming tables and the brass swinging green shaded lights could have been in any gambling house. And so could the crowd of ranchers. The difference was that there were no professional gamblers. And then there were the deputies guarding the joint with a bunch of silver derringers. And there were no women—not a dove or a barmaid in sight.

Mort Murphy entered with Ruby on his arm. Today she wore a high-necked red day dress which clung to her every rounded curve. She spotted him and waved, approaching the table.

"Isn't it wonderful?" she asked Fargo, gesturing around the room. "Even in the daytime, there are plenty of customers." She looked up proudly at Mort, who loomed over their table.

"How come there are no women around?" Fargo asked. It was an indelicate question to put to Mort in the presence of his sister, but hell, he knew from firsthand experience Ruby Murphy wasn't exactly the innocent type.

"What a question!" Ruby said indignantly. "My brother runs a clean place."

"I made the decision that the Blackgulch Gaming House ought to be kind of a family place," Mort said, looking down at Fargo. "Good clean fun, just a little gambling and drinking. Nothing you couldn't go home and tell your wife about. That's the kind of place Blackgulch deserves."

It was an odd answer, Fargo thought. But then as he thought about it, he realized how smart Mort Murphy was. He remembered the way he'd been so solicitous of Mrs. Hawkins on the street and how highly she thought of him in return. Of course. With no doves to make the wives jealous and with Mort Murphy ingratiating himself with all the ranchers' spouses, the women wouldn't complain when their husbands spent time at the casino. Sure, it made perfect business sense.

The Murphys left and Leatherberry was itching to watch the action so they wandered over to one of the tables where a game of twenty-one was taking place, an older rancher playing against the house. Time after time, the man seemed to get close with two tens or a jack and an eight, only to lose out to the dealer. The man's stack of chips was getting lower and lower until finally, he played his last and lost.

"Guess I gotta quit," the man said. "I'm plumb outta cash."

"The house can advance you," the dealer said kindly, his black eyes glittering.

"Oh, no," the old man said. "I'm so advanced on the casino, I ain't never going to win it back. Hell—"

"You're just waiting for your luck to turn. Here, let's try one hand. I'll advance you the chips."

The dealer tossed two chips onto the table in front of the old man, then dealt out the hand. The old man struck twenty-one and then had four chips. He won a second time, bet them all then lost the third. By now, he was so excited, he took the dealer up on the offer of an advance.

"You're on a roll," the dealer said. "Just sign here." From under the table, the dealer pulled a notebook and opened it to a page. There was a long list of signatures all alike. The man signed again, received a huge pile of chips and promptly began losing them again. Fargo and Leatherberry moved off, the small gambling man shaking his head in disgust.

For the next several hours they stopped to watch games of poker and roulette, faro and chuck-a-luck, and always it was the same thing. The ranchers losing and losing. The dealers pressuring them to sign over for more advances. Clearly everybody was in debt to the casino and with every roll of the dice, it seemed to get worse.

Then in late afternoon, the hubbub around a table drew them and they watched a faro game played by Al Hawkins. Card after card, luck was completely with him and the stack of chips in front of him rose higher and higher as the crowd gathered, breathlessly awaiting every hand.

"That's it!" Hawkins said at last. "I got a thousand dollars here! I'm going to cash in!"

The crowd roared its approval and drifted away to the other games. Fargo couldn't help but notice that the success Hawkins had had seemed to make the other ranchers all the more eager to lay down their bets. As he was gathering up his chips, the dealer was talking to Hawkins.

"What about half?" the dealer asked smoothly. "Remember, you could double your money. And if you lose, you still got five hundred dollars. Just give it one chance. After all, this seems to be your lucky day. It would be a shame to stop now."

Fargo saw Hawkins hesitate for just a moment. Then he relented, put down his money on the table and the dealer dealt again. As he could have predicted, in twenty minutes the thousand dollars belonged to the Blackgulch Gaming House again and Al Hawkins sat glumly at the table with his head in his hands.

"This is the worse setup I've ever seen," Leatherberry said quietly. "The casino is in complete control, with all the odds in their favor, and the rubes don't even know it."

"Every single man here is probably bankrupt and owing the casino," Fargo mused.

"Damn right," Leatherberry said. "Of course, I could beat this house. I mean, a few shuffles and—"

"Well don't," Fargo said. "Not tonight anyhow.

All I need is for you to get thrown out of the casino. We need to play this low-key."

"All right, all right," Leatherberry said, feigning disappointment. "Wouldn't be much of a challenge anyhow."

"We need to keep our eyes open. I still haven't figured out who kidnapped Ruby and what the connection is with the casino. There's a lot I don't understand about this town."

A few hours later, they were standing beside the bar near the door when Al Hawkins staggered by. It was clear that the rancher had been drinking heavily ever since he had won and then lost the thousand dollars to the casino. He bumped into Fargo.

"'Scuse me," he muttered, then turned and peered into his face, bleary-eyed. "Did I see you somewhere before? In here yesterday, maybe?"

Al Hawkins' voice was loud and drunken, but not hostile.

"Maybe," Fargo said affably.

"The name's Al Hawkins," the drunken man said. "And who are you?"

When Fargo said his name, the man's face darkened and turned purple. He took a step backward and shook his head to clear it.

"What the hell are you doing here?" Hawkins asked.

"Oh, I guess you could say I delivered Mort Murphy's sister back to him," Fargo said, taking a sip of beer. He introduced Josh Leatherberry, of whom Hawkins took no notice.

"Lemme get this . . . this straight. You're—you're *working* for Mort Murphy?" Al Hawkins said, sounding incredulous.

"Not really—" Fargo said.

Al Hawkins didn't wait for the answer but reeled again, held himself from falling with one hand on the bar. Then the man staggered off toward the door, mumbling angrily.

It was almost midnight by the time they'd had enough. Increasingly, all evening Fargo had had the vague sensation he was being watched, being looked at. Time and time again he looked up to find one of the ranchers darting him an angry look or just turning his eyes away. The feeling persisted as they retrieved their guns and went outside.

"No wonder there aren't any professional gamblers in Blackgulch," Leatherberry said as they walked up the street toward the hotel. "No gambler worth his chips would put up with those kind of odds. Why, that casino is just downright *stealing* from those poor dumb bastards. They don't have a chance."

Mort Murphy must be a very rich man, Fargo thought. But what was it that Mort really wanted? Fargo had the feeling that if it were only money, Murphy would have set up a casino in one of the big towns or in a place where lots of well-heeled high rollers would come. But instead, he had settled on Blackgulch. Why?

They reached the hotel and entered. The old man was asleep—again—at the front desk. They climbed the stairs and said good night. Leatherberry entered his room but just outside his door, Fargo paused. His instincts told him something was wrong. That there was somebody waiting inside the room. Maybe. He quietly moved to Leatherberry's door and tapped. The gambler appeared, his face surprised. Fargo explained the situation. Immediately, Leatherberry understood and began talking in a loud voice.

"Sure, come on in Fargo. Sit down over here."

Leatherberry closed his door and continued talking as Fargo moved off silently down the hall. It sounded like a couple of men inside the room. In a few minutes, Fargo had exited the hotel, climbed up onto the sloping tin roof of the front porch and was slowly creeping his way across to his darkened hotel window. Through the next window, which was lighted, he heard Leatherberry chattering on. He slid the Colt out of his holster as he eased himself up to peer into his room, expecting to see the dark figures of men waiting for his return, ready to jump him.

What he saw was worse.

In the empty darkened room, hanging from the beam, was the form of a man, swinging slowly back and forth from a hangman's noose.

5

The dark figure swung back and forth above the bed in the dark hotel room, hanged by the neck. Who the hell was he? Fargo, balanced on the tin roof, peered through the pane, his eyes searching for anyone else in his room. Was there someone waiting to jump him? But there was no one, although the bureau drawers had been searched and the chair overturned and the mirror smashed. He eased up the windowsash and climbed into the disheveled room.

Instantly, he saw he'd been mistaken. What he thought was a dead man was only clothing stuffed to look like a figure. But it was his clothing. He tapped an all-clear signal on the wall to alert Leatherberry, who appeared at the door a moment later.

"Who the hell—?" Leatherberry gasped as he entered the darkened room a moment before he recognized the figure as only an effigy.

Fargo lit the oil lamp and spun the figure around. There was a message pinned to the front of the shirt: "GET OUT OF TOWN, TRAILSMAN,

MONEY-GRUBBING DOUBLE-CROSSING BASTARD. GET OUT OF THE COUNTY BEFORE THE NEXT SUNDOWN OR WE'LL HANG YOU TOO."

"Looks like you've got an enemy," Leatherberry said. "Must be Bo Boggs."

Fargo thought as he untied the figure and took the pillows and sheets out of his clothing, dismantling the dummy.

"I don't think so. It just doesn't seem like something Boggs would do."

"Yeah," Leatherberry agreed. "Well maybe it's the whole posse of deputies."

"Maybe," Fargo said doubtfully. "But I wonder what they meant by double-crossing?"

"And money-grubbing?"

Fargo felt about in his inside vest pocket and pulled out the telegram, the garbled message that had reached him after so many months in New Orleans. Once again, he scanned the nonsense letters, trying to make sense of them. But the only word he could read was *Blackgulch*. Maybe the threat had to do with this telegram. He just needed more information. There was something going on in this town that he still didn't understand. It had to do with Mort Murphy and his casino, with whatever it was that Ruby had been trying to find out back on the riverboat. The ranchers were involved too and so were Lars Hulbert and his gang of ruffian deputies.

"The problem is, there's nobody I can ask . . ." Fargo muttered, talking aloud to himself.

"Yeah, everybody in this town seems to be keeping some kind of secret," Leatherberry said, as if he had followed Fargo's train of thought completely.

Then Fargo remembered Paul Cahill and his daughter Betsy. Maybe the rancher would divulge some information that would make sense of the whole thing. The more he thought about it, the more he felt sure Cahill could be of help to him. He explained his plan to Leatherberry, who would stay behind in Blackgulch and keep an eye on happenings at the casino and keep his ears open for any talk.

After a sound sleep and a good breakfast, Fargo made a show of bringing the Ovaro around to the front of the hotel. He checked out and loaded his gear into his saddlebags. A few passersby saw him and he knew word would get around town that he'd left. Let whoever left the message for him think that he'd been scared off. Maybe that way, they'd drop their guard.

On his way out of town, he dropped in on the casino and found Mort Murphy in his office.

Under the green-shaded lamp, the tall man sat behind his massive gleaming desk. He was drinking a cup of coffee and poring over the ledgers, a grin on his face. As Fargo walked in, Mort looked up, started in surprise, then hastily covered up the papers. He rose to his feet and put on a wide smile. But in one glance, Fargo had seen a little of the ledgers, had noticed that all the way down the page were names and next to them were numbers—large numbers, each preceded by a red minus mark.

"Just came to say good-bye," Fargo said. "I'm heading out."

"Sorry to see you go," Murphy said, sounding anything but. Fargo waited, wondering if Murphy would add any comment that might indicate he knew anything about the hanged dummy and the warning left in his hotel room. But Mort stood silently.

"Is Ruby around?" He didn't really care to see her, but maybe Mort would leave the room and he could get another look at the ledgers.

"She's having her bath." He continued to stand behind the desk, one hand on the stack of papers.

"Tell her I stopped in," Fargo said as he left.

The morning sun and the washed-out cloudless sky promised a hot day. He swung onto the saddle, glad to feel the strength of the black-and-white pinto under him again. The horse was eager to be off, galloping across the open lands. Fargo kept the pinto at a slow walk through town. Knots of women were gathered on the boardwalks, directing their husbands, who had climbed up on the roofs of the buildings and were stringing up the red, white, and blue bunting for the July Fourth celebration, only days away. He waved as he passed so that as many people as possible would notice him riding out and word would get around.

Just outside town, he found a narrow track of wagon wheels that led northeast, winding over the gentle rises through the green grassland that was just starting to turn gold in the heat of summer. He felt the embrace of the wide open plains as if it welcomed the bounding gallop of his horse beneath the exhilarating freedom of the seemingly endless expanse of clear blue sky. He gave the Ovaro free rein and it sped along the trail, gleaming sweat in the sun, lathering with foam. The trail descended to a creek where the cottonwoods rose like parasols, their leaves quivering and glittering in the sun. The wind in the trees sounded like rushing water, louder than the noise of the burbling creek where the pinto paused for a drink.

This must be Sawtooth Creek, in which case he might already be on Cahill land. On the other side of the creek, he found a stake with the mark of the Flying C Ranch, marking the boundary of the spread. In another mile, he spotted a cattle wallow, red soil and opaque red water surrounded by the scruffy bunchgrass that had been chewed low by the grazing longhorns. The mud was dimpled deep by their hooves.

Just over the hill, part of the herd was grazing and he spotted three cowpokes on horses poised on the rise of the next hill. These, he knew, would be the line-riders, the hands that had the grueling duty of guarding the perimeter of the huge ranch, riding mile after mile to keep an eye on the movements of the herd to make sure it didn't break apart or wander off and also to make sure no unwelcome visitors—such as rustlers—wandered in.

As Fargo cantered toward the three, he noticed they seemed to be huddled together discussing something. Finally, one broke out from the group and rode toward him, reining in his sleek gray as he came within a few yards.

The cowpoke's hat had blown back off his head and hung by its strap. He was a young kid, freckle-faced, carrot-topped, and cow-licked. And, Fargo was surprised to see, scared. Scared out of his mind. The kid's hand twitched as if he wanted to put it on the rifle that poked out of the saddle scabbard. The other two cowpokes were watching closely from the hill. And their hands were resting on their rifles.

"I'm looking for Paul Cahill," Fargo said.

"This is the Flying C," the kid said hesitantly. "What's your business with Mr. Cahill?"

While normally Fargo would have taken offense at the kid's nosy question, in this case he figured there must be some trouble and the kid was trying to protect his boss.

"He invited me to come over. The name's Skye Fargo."

The kid had obviously heard the stories about him because his eyes got wide and he broke out in a wide grin.

"I'm Stevie Border," the kid said excitedly. "Nice to meet you, Mr. Fargo. I'll take you to Mr. Cahill. Follow me."

The Ovaro refused to follow the gray, but overtook it, then matched its stride as they galloped down the incline, then up the hill where the two others waited. The kid, Stevie, scarcely paused but shouted out his errand to his compatriots as he sped past. They galloped side by side another few miles until they spotted a chuck wagon and a few horses tethered there.

As they pulled up, a knot of men broke apart and Fargo dismounted as the familiar stocky figure of Paul Cahill came walking toward him.

"Fargo!" the rancher called out, his green eyes alight. Once again, Fargo was struck by the impression of the man's thick-shouldered steadiness. "Welcome to the Flying C."

Cahill shook hands warmly with him, introduced him to the other ranchhands standing around, who were all impressed by his reputation. Stevie Border was reluctant to get back to his post and skittered around between the older men like an excited puppy dog. Finally, one of the hands sent the kid back to the other line-riders.

The hot sun was high overhead when Paul Cahill and Fargo rode off toward the ranch house for the noonday meal. As they rode at an easy pace, Fargo admired the spreading land and the herd.

"We're all damn lucky with these Texas longhorns," Paul Cahill said as they trotted along. "They're hardy, they're nimble, and they drink a helluva lot less water than those fat cows back East. Of course, they got less beef on 'em too, but what they got is enough."

"You tried raising any Eastern cattle out here?" Fargo asked.

"Interesting question," Cahill replied. "I knew a rancher who did but they all died of disease, drought, insect bites, and just plain heat. I got the idea to breed some longhorns with some blooded

Durhams. That way I'll get hardy stock that's also beef-rich. I started doing it last year and I think that's going to be the future of our Texas cattle."

The rancher sounded very excited about his plans, Fargo noted. So different from the resigned, dejected man who had not even wanted to pursue Bo Boggs and Lars Hulbert, despite the assault on his daughter.

"Sounds like your ranch is doing well," Fargo said.

"Well—" Paul Cahill sounded hesitant for a moment, then continued as if talking to convince himself—"if a man's lucky, his herd doubles every three years and you can get almost ten bucks a head. And it only takes one cowhand to tend a thousand head. Ranching can be a fine business. A man can do well. If he's lucky."

The ranchhouse came into view, a modest compound of stables, barns, corrals, watering troughs, all surrounding a spreading comfortable-looking house collared with a shady porch. They dismounted, unsaddled the horses, penned them and went inside.

"Betsy! Betsy! We got a guest!" Paul Cahill called out.

The house inside was modest but well appointed with woven wool rugs on the floors and hung on the walls, thick furniture made of logs, and a huge stone fireplace that dominated the great room. A few trophy heads of bears and elk were hung along one wall.

Betsy appeared wearing a leather skirt and a

white shirt, both of which accentuated her long slender form. Her honey hair was tied back and her brown eyes opened in surprise as she recognized him.

"Skye!" she said. "I mean, Mr. Fargo."

"Skye, please," he insisted.

She stood blinking her eyes at him, as if not believing he was there and for a moment, there was an awkward silence. She blushed.

"Well, how about some lunch?" Paul cut in.

Betsy seemed to come out of her reverie and she ducked back into the kitchen, glancing back over her shoulder at him.

They sat at a wooden table in the shade of the porch while Betsy brought out heaps of sliced beef, Indian bread, and bowls of corn pudding and sliced tomatoes. The afternoon breeze kept them cool but across the distance the heat rose in waves.

As they talked, Paul Cahill gave the impression that everything was fine at his ranch. And yet, Fargo saw that each time her father spoke, Betsy became more and more angry.

"Why don't you tell Skye what's really been going on here?" she finally exploded.

"Now, Betsy," Cahill said, "we gotta solve our own problems."

"You're just too proud to ask for help," she said angrily.

"What is the trouble?" he asked her directly.

"Rustlers," she said. "For the last few weeks, every couple of nights they ride through. They drove off some of the herd. And so far, our boys haven't been able to catch up with them. The ranch is just too big to be everywhere at once. Then a few weeks ago, they shot and killed one of our hands. Another got shot in the leg a couple of nights ago. Three of our hired help quit the next day. And if those rustlers come back and shoot anybody else, I'm afraid we'll lose every one of those boys. And it's hard to find good cowpokes these days."

Paul Cahill looked embarrassed.

"We ain't asking for your help in this," the rancher said, looking down at his plate. "Seems like everybody in the world must ask you for help, only we're not."

"How about the other ranchers hereabouts?" Fargo cut in. Usually, when there were rustlers in the neighborhood, ranchers banded together and put up a special posse.

"Well, that's the funny thing," Betsy said. "These rustlers are only visiting the Flying C. Nobody else has had any trouble whatsoever?"

"How many cattle have you been missing?"

"Only about fifty head so far," Betsy said. "Most of them either wandered back home or the boys found them halfway to kingdom come and brought them back."

"I don't know if I can help you, but I'll try," he said.

"We couldn't afford your fee," Paul Cahill put in. "I've heard you charge top dollar." Fargo thought about the note on the dummy in his hotel room and wondered if just possibly Paul Cahill had anything to do with it. He decided to see.

"You mean I'm money-grubbing?"

"I didn't mean it like that," Cahill said with a wince. "I didn't mean to give offense." Fargo, watching Cahill's face carefully, didn't see any sign of recognition there or any guilt or deceit.

"I'll do the job in exchange for some information," Fargo said. "Just answer some questions."

"I doubt I know anything that would be useful to you," Cahill said. He looked a little nervous.

"It seems to me everybody in Blackgulch is hiding something," Fargo said. "Only I can't make out exactly what it is—"

"Gambling debts," Paul Cahill put in immediately. "Every rancher in this county except for me spends his time at Mort Murphy's den of iniquity. And every single one of them is in debt up to his eyeballs and hiding it from his wife and his family. And every rancher goes back there like a damn fool trying to win some money back. By now, all of them are so deep in it, they've signed over their ranches, their herds, and probably everything else they own. The only thing that keeps the whole town from collapse is that Mort Murphy hasn't called in their debts yet. He's floating the whole town of Blackgulch and the ranches too."

Of course. Those were the figures in the ledger that Fargo had glimpsed in Mort Murphy's office. And he remembered how, in the casino, every time a player ran out of chips and ran out of money, the house was eager to advance him, the dealers cajoling them to sign away another part of their property.

"And the worst part of it," Paul Cahill said, "is that it's all perfectly legal. Every document that Mort Murphy had those ranchers sign was prepared by a fancy lawyer back East and they are iron-clad. Mort Murphy has won, fair and square. He's got the law on his side."

"In more ways than one," Fargo said. "He appears to own Lars Hulbert, lock, stock, and barrel."

"Absolutely," Cahill said. "The sheriff is in Murphy's pocket, and Murphy himself pays the salaries of all those thugs they call deputies. The whole town stinks with them."

"It's not fair," Betsy said hotly.

"I agree," Fargo said. "But the ranchers bear some of the responsibility. Any grown man ought to know it's more likely than not he's going to lose when he gambles. So, those men are getting some of what they deserve. But, even so, it sounds like Murphy has been on a determined campaign to ruin every one of them."

"Exactly what I've been thinking," Paul Cahill said. "But why would he want to do that?"

"He just wants to get richer," Betsy said.

"Maybe," Fargo said. But he felt there was more to Mort Murphy's motives than that. He'd seen the man in action and he was complex, dangerous. And then there was Ruby. That reminded him of the telegram and he fished it from his pocket, showed it to them, and explained how he received it. Betsy took it and tried to decipher the mixed-up letters, but then gave up and watched as Fargo folded it and put it back in his vest pocket.

"Yeah, I got an idea that the men of Blackgulch sent it," Cahill said. "To tell you the truth, they've all been getting desperate. None of their wives know any of this is going on, because they all think Mort Murphy walks on water. But way last spring, three or four months ago, Al Hawkins was talking some big talk that he'd figured out a way to get things put right again and he'd found just the man for the job. Then he never said anything more about it."

Fargo remembered running into Al Hawkins the night before, drunk in the casino, and how angry the rancher had been to learn his identity and how he had accused Fargo of working for Murphy. Yeah, it all made sense now. Hawkins had figured that Fargo had not bothered to reply to his telegram and had hired himself out to the casino owner in order to make even more money than the ranchers could afford to pay. And Hawkins and some of his friends had probably also left the effigy in Fargo's hotel room, angry at what they thought was a double-cross.

He rose from the table and paced back and forth on the porch, deep in thought as the Cahills watched him. Yeah, he could see it pretty clearly now. But what the hell was he going to do to stop Mort Murphy? And now he'd promised the Cahills to help them out with the rustlers.

"You look like you need a ride," Cahill said. "Why don't you take a gallop north up to the Indian River. Pretty up that way."

"I'll take him, Pa," Betsy said eagerly. "Big Red could use some exercise."

In fifteen minutes, they had the horses saddled and they were off.

Betsy rode well, a true rancher, easy on her horse, her slender body moving in perfect rhythm with the powerful gait of her long-legged red. Her honey hair came loose and flowed behind her in the wind. They raced up and down the hills, Betsy laughing with delight. Fargo held the Ovaro slightly in check so it wouldn't leave Betsy's red too far behind.

The afternoon was golden and hot, the sun sinking by slow degrees in the blue cloudless sky. They passed groups of cowpokes tending parts of the Cahill herd. There were plenty of calves and the longhorns were as healthy and well fed as any he'd ever seen. From what Fargo could see, it looked as if the Flying C would have a good year if they could get all those beeves up to the market.

By midafternoon, they had reached the Indian River. Its wide yellow current had sloping banks shaded by tall cottonwood trees and chokecherry thickets. They dismounted and let the horses drink. Fargo fetched the canteen from his saddlebag and offered it to Betsy, who was combing the tangles out of her long honey hair. It gleamed in the sunlight.

She took a few swigs, then poured some in her hand and patted it on her throat to cool down. Her shirt had come unbuttoned and he could see a small rounded breast tipped with a dark erect nipple. She followed his gaze.

"I understand that . . ." she blushed and left the rest of her sentence unsaid, her eyes looking across the river. Fargo knew what she was thinking. She was thinking of what had happened back in the stable in Blackgulch.

"I thought you were very beautiful," he said.

She turned to face him and he took her in his arms, pulled her to him as she came, willing, wanting. Her mouth was warm, welcoming, sweet. His hands found her small frame, the narrow hips and rib cage, her back, the small breasts that fit into his palm. She shivered under his touch, her breath panting.

"Here?" he asked. She nodded.

He pulled a blanket out of the saddlebag and laid it out on a grassy bank. She lay down, suddenly shy as he stretched out beside her. Her lean body was lovely and he imagined her without her clothes. Her honey hair was strewn around her face on the pillow and her liquid brown eyes were filled with want. The breeze blew gently, the leaves of the cottonwoods rustled overhead and birds sang.

Slowly, he traced a line down her slender throat with one finger, lightly as a feather. She shivered at his touch, looking upward at the trees, too shy to catch his eye. She moved her hand to the buttons of her shirt, as if telling him what she wanted, and he began slowly to unbutton her, pulling the fabric back to reveal her breasts. Her skin had a honey tone, her nipples were dark and crinkled with desire, like ripe berries. He covered one with his mouth, taking the nipple gently between his lips, then tonguing it in circles, slowly, then faster.

Betsy moaned low and he felt her hips begin to move eagerly. He slowly moved his hand along her narrow side until he found the mound of her beneath her leather skirt. He pressed against her, felt her body arc to come to meet his hand. As he kissed her, her knees came up and he found the hem of her skirt, then the warm satin of her inner thigh, inch by inch, until he brushed against her undergarments, pulled them aside to find the warm fur, the slick wetness of her. He was rock hard, throbbing and wanting.

He sat up and she looked surprised. He gently pulled down her undergarment as she helped him, struggling out of them. Then he firmly parted her legs with his hands, opening her thighs, her skirt sliding upward. He glimpsed the golden tangle there, the moist pink folds of her. She looked as though she didn't know what he was about to do. She giggled when he kissed her bent knee, then continued, his tongue trailing upward slowly until he reached her pink swollen lips, inhaled the warm fragrant musk of her.

"Oh, oh! Skye, oh please, yes . . ." Betsy said as his tongue flicked her tenderness. He took her completely into his mouth, sucking gently. She was going wild with desire. With the tip of his insistent tongue he sought the hard seed of her, found it buried in the sweet fruit, and sucked, gently then harder as she bucked under him. He could feel the wave of pleasure he was giving her, making his cock harder and harder, throbbing and eager.

He could hardly wait to be inside her and then she came, explosively, crying out and shuddering all over and he pulled back, kneeling between her legs, lowered his jeans. His prick stood out, heavy and hard and ready, aching for her.

"Yes, yes, now," she said, grasping him in one cool hand and opening wider to him as he plunged between her thighs, feeling the last shudders of her orgasm, thrusting upward into the warm depth of her, the sliding hot tightness of her pussy. Her knees came up around him and he thrust in, deep, then shallow, then deep again. She moaned with pleasure and he kissed her mouth, her eyelids, her throat, covered her sweet breasts with his hands as he pushed, deeper into her, feeling the gathering in him, the explosion, the fountain about to erupt, and then came the urgent thrusts, the waves of pleasure that coursed through him like electricity as her narrow hips met his, thrust for thrust, and then he came, pumping and hot, as the world spun around him and there was only this woman beneath him, around him, driving into her and coming, coming, until he was dry and spent.

Afterward, they lay together side by side. They napped for a while and when he woke, he found her curled against him, her eyes closed. She was lovely. He stroked her long slender form and she awakened slowly, smiled at him.

"Oh, Skye, that was wonderful," she whispered in his ear. He pulled her toward him, kissing her and feeling the warmth of her nakedness against him, the slight mint odor of her skin, and his hand brushed against her thigh, found again the wet folds of her.

"Want to come again?" he asked, stroking her with his fingers, teasing her and rubbing her.

"Ah," she said as she kissed him, her tongue plunging into his mouth, swirling around his. His finger entered her, then another, then he rubbed her again, felt the hard knot of her tightening as she tensed, ready again, and then she slipped over the brink with a cry, delicately. And he found he was ready for her again and entered her, slowly this time, easing into her wet warmth and stroking slowly, then faster as she held him in an embrace, smiling up at him as he gave himself to her a second time, coming less urgently this time, shooting up into her arcing slender body until he was exhausted.

Afterward they rose and bathed in the yellow water. Betsy Cahill, naked in the afternoon light, her slender grace against the water, looked like a nymph in an old storybook. They dried off with a cotton blanket from the saddlebag and got dressed.

Suddenly, he noticed she wouldn't catch his eye as she got her horse saddled and he grabbed her hand and pulled her toward him. He could see the hesitancy in her face.

"You know I'm not the settling kind," he said. She nodded. "But as long as you're willing, I'd like to do that again. As long as I'm around. You're a beautiful woman, Betsy."

She smiled at him and he kissed her again. They mounted and rode off toward the south, the horses in an easy canter. The sun was touching down on the horizon. They had gone only a mile or two when they spotted a campfire on a distant rise.

Betsy angled off that direction to check on the cowpokes and Fargo followed. They arrived to find some of the line-riders, about ten of them, making a camp for the night and cooking up a pot of chili. The hands invited Betsy and Fargo to join them. The sun turned orange, then red, and sank in a bank of fiery clouds. The stars came out overhead and around them they could hear the herd settling down for the night. The cowpokes took turns going to check on the cattle.

The rest sat around the campfire. The grub was good—trail food usually was—and afterward, the cowpokes built up the campfire and brought out their harmonicas and sang some old songs. The kid named Stevie Border was there and he wanted Fargo to tell some of his stories, which he did, at least the parts of them he could tell in mixed company. The cowpokes hung on his every word. The moon began to rise and it was time to head back to the ranchhouse.

Fargo had just approached the Ovaro when he sensed there was something wrong. The horse felt it too, its ears flicking back and forth. It moved from one foot to the other, restlessly. Fargo looked out across the moonlit land, searching with his keen eyes and with that sixth sense that the years of living in the wild had bred into him. He could hear nothing over the singing of the cowpokes a short distance away by the fire. Betsy brought up her horse, then noticed his attention.

"Is something wrong?"

"Yeah. But I don't know what it is yet."

He continued to stand watching, waiting. The Ovaro neighed low. Yeah, he was certain now. Certain. Movement out on the land. Riders. His eyes could hardly discern them in the darkness but somehow he knew they were out there. He returned to the campfire and told the cowpokes to saddle up. They spent a few minutes arranging their sleeping blankets spread over rocks and logs to make it look like they were all asleep around the fire. Then Fargo led them to a position just outside the circle of firelight and they sat waiting, listening, and watching. After a while, he knew he was right and he also knew the riders were heading straight for them, drawn by the golden flicker of the campfire.

The cowpokes were scared all right. Most of them weren't much older than Stevie Border and they'd signed up for a life of herding cattle, not facing down gun-toting rustlers in the middle of the night.

So Fargo told them his plan, how they would form a huge open V with the campfire at the apex, staying well back in the dark. Then they would let the riders come in close, between them and the fire, and at Fargo's signal—three shots in rapid succession—they would close the V, surround the rustlers and the campfire.

The cowpokes took their positions and Fargo, with Betsy at his side, rode along the line, making sure everyone was in place. Then Fargo sent Betsy to a position well back of the line at the point of the V and he rode to the very front.

He had just reined in and sat silent and still on the Ovaro when the riders came rushing over the next rise. There were about a dozen of them, he saw with relief, so they were almost evenly matched. The riders galloped by in the darkness, too far away for him to see anything of them. As the last of them passed, Fargo brought the Ovaro slowly forward and signaled to the next man in line to begin closing the formation.

In a minute, the rustlers pulled up in the darkness and reconnoitered the camp. It looked like everybody was asleep. Instantly, the riders rode straight in, guns blazing, shooting at the rocks and logs wrapped in blankets. Fargo brought the Ovaro forward now in a gallop. In the darkness, he saw the other cowpokes closing in to form a circle around the unsuspecting rustlers, who continued to shoot, riding right into the camp. Fargo drew the Colt and raised it above his head, squeezed off one, two, three sudden shots. And the gunfire erupted from all sides, pouring into the clearing and catching the rustlers by complete surprise.

Their reaction was instantaneous. Several horses reared and two of the riders were thrown. As one tried to crawl behind a rock, Fargo plugged him in the ribs and he collapsed and lay still. Others tried to ride out, to break through the line, but their eyes were dazzled by the campfire and they couldn't see the ranchhands in the blackness.

Bullets whizzed and guns exploded. Most of the rustlers were shot in the first onslaught, but four had managed to get off their horses and hunker down under cover in the camp. The ones who tried to break the line were shot dead. After a few more minutes, it became obvious the battle was won. Fargo saw a white handkerchief on a stick being waved in the light of the fire.

He called a halt to the shooting. The cowpokes gave a loud cheer in the sudden silence, then moved forward in a tightening circle. Fargo rode forward slowly among the others.

"We did it!" Stevie Border crowed. "We beat them rustlers."

Fargo silenced the kid with a stern look.

"Get your hands in the air!" he instructed. Three pairs of hands appeared from various hiding places behind rocks and logs. Fargo thought for a moment there had been four. But in the heat of battle, it had been impossible to tell for sure.

"All right, throw your guns toward the fire."

The three men threw two rifles and a pistol near the fire.

"All your weapons," he added. There was a pause and then another rifle and two pistols were tossed toward the fire.

"All right, let's see your hands again. Get to your feet."

The three men rose.

"Why, those men are deputies!" Stevie Border said in astonishment.

"All right, tie them up," Fargo said to two of the ranchhands. They did as he ordered. "Where are your tin stars?" Fargo asked as he strode forward. "As lawmen you ought to know that rustling is a hanging offense in these parts. We could just string you up here and now."

"Hell, we weren't rustling cattle," one muttered. "We was just supposed to be scaring 'em off."

"By killing the ranchhands. Killing's a hanging crime too and you've killed one of the Flying C ranchhands already."

The three men shifted nervously beneath his gaze. Betsy Cahill came riding up. She dismounted and was shocked to see the three of Lars Hulbert's men standing there. Fargo walked back and forth in front of the three men.

"Did the sheriff order you to do this?" He grabbed the collar of one of the men and shook him, shouting at him nose to nose. "Answer me!" The man flinched.

"Well, Mr. Murphy does the ordering. And the sheriff does what he's told. And so do we."

Betsy Cahill was walking around the campsite nervously. She approached the grub wagon. Fargo saw a sudden flurry of movement there. Too late, Fargo realized that the fourth man had hidden in the grub wagon. Suddenly, a huge form vaulted down from the wagon and grabbed Betsy. She screamed and Fargo cursed. It was Bo Boggs and as he wrapped his huge arms around her slender form, he had a pistol aimed right at Betsy Cahill's head and his finger was tight on the trigger.

There was no need for words. Bo Boggs' intentions were clear. If they didn't let him out of camp, he'd shoot her dead. The cowpokes watched in dread as Bo Boggs edged along in the firelight. He was limping, the thigh where Fargo had shot him must hurt like hell. Fargo stood with his Colt in hand, hoping Boggs would stumble, make one bad move, give him a clear shot, but he held Betsy Cahill in front of him and as long as that was the case, there was nothing Fargo could do.

The nearest standing horse was the black-and-white pinto. Boggs spotted it and edged toward it. Fargo waited until Boggs was within a few feet, then he puckered his lips and whistled low. The Ovaro reared up and Boggs whirled about. Betsy Cahill fell to the ground just as the pinto's mighty hooves came down on Bo Boggs' shoulders and chest. He went down.

Fargo rushed in, pushed Betsy further away and into cover behind some rocks, then stood over Boggs, who was lying facedown on the ground. He wasn't moving. Fargo approached to within a step of the man and suddenly Boggs rolled over, his gun in hand and spitting fire.

But Fargo was too quick. He pulled the trigger of the Colt and a dark hole appeared on Boggs' forehead between his two eyebrows. Boggs looked surprised for a moment, then the expression faded and he was gone. A dark stream of blood ran down the side of his face.

"Hell, you didn't have to go and shoot Boggs," one of the deputies muttered. Fargo pointed the Colt at the man and cocked the trigger. "Is that all of them?" he called out. "Search the camp and let's make sure."

The cowpokes did and it seemed they had got all the rustlers. Fargo noticed that the kid wasn't crowing anymore, but had set to work searching the camp and helping to tie up the prisoners more securely. The three that were trussed like chickens lay in a row by the fire which had cooled to red embers.

Then suddenly, the cold night wind shifted and he smelled woodsmoke. Not the nearby char of their campfire, but a deep burning smell from far away. He scanned the horizon and saw what he feared.

There in the night sky was a red glow. It was the ranchhouse. The rustlers were burning it down.

Betsy Cahill spotted the fire at the same instant he did.

"Pa! Pa!" she screamed. She raced for her horse, mounted, and was galloping off into the darkness before he hardly had a chance to move.

6

The sound of the hoofbeats of Betsy's horse disappeared in the direction of the burning ranch house. The ranchhands moved aimlessly around the campfire, not knowing what to do.

"Keep an eye on these men," Fargo shouted to them, "and when you come to the ranchhouse, ride in a group, guns at the ready. There's no telling how many of Hulbert's deputies are out there tonight."

Fargo leapt onto the Ovaro and pursued Betsy. He caught up to her in just half a mile. Her red was going full-out down the trail. She was giving it the quirt and it was running as if chased by the devil himself. But even so, it was no match for the powerful gait of the Ovaro.

He brought his horse alongside hers. Her hair was wild and her face hard set. He could tell immediately she was riding in a panic, thoughtlessly. Always a dangerous thing to do. A rider could get tossed and killed riding that way. He edged closer as their two mounts pounded the hard-packed trail. Then he reached over and grasped the reins of her red, pulling it in a little.

"Pa needs me!"

"He needs you alive!"

The words seemed to sink in and Betsy pulled up a little. The red was still galloping hard, but less foolhardedly. They concentrated on the riding, wasting no effort on words.

The sharp odor of woodsmoke grew stronger and the red glow widened in the sky until he could see a pillar of smoke billowing up into the cloudless night, obscuring the stars and lit by the fire as if right out of Hell.

They came to within sight of the ranch. He was expecting to see a gun battle raging. But instead, whoever had set the fire had apparently ridden off. The ranchhands were running to and fro trying to put out the fire.

They galloped into the compound and dismounted. The ranch house was ablaze, as was the storehouse. The barn suddenly lit up—obviously the dry hay had just caught fire. Fargo heard the terrified screams of animals, a sound more awful than almost anything he could think of.

Before he could move toward it, the Ovaro reared, came about, and plunged straight at the barn. It came up on its hind legs and pounded at the barn doors with its powerful forelegs until the doors gave way, collapsing inward. Gray smoke came billowing out. Four horses came racing out of the burning barn along with several chickens and pigs.

"Where's Pa? Where's Pa?"

Betsy Cahill was frantic as she ran among the cowhands.

"He must be out on the spread!" one of them shouted back.

"We haven't seen him!"

Betsy Cahill stood twisting her hands, the flickering fire lighting her face. She looked toward the ranch house. Suddenly, she let out a piercing scream.

"He's in there! I know he is!"

She ran straight for the burning building. Fargo dashed after her, barely managing to pull her back from the burning porch. She fought him, pounded him with her fists in a fury of fright.

"He's in there! Pa's in there, I just know he is!"

Fargo glanced at the burning ranch house. Hell, it was possible Paul Cahill was inside. The structure was crackling and snapping, the dry wood exploding with flames, threatening to collapse at any moment.

"Let me go! Let me go!" Betsy Cahill had turned into a spitting animal in her horror. She was convinced her father was inside. Sometimes people had instincts about certain things. Hell, she might be right. Maybe he ought to go in for one quick look. But what if she were wrong and he risked or lost his life for nothing? But something told him—his own instinct—that Betsy Cahill was right.

"I'll go!" he shouted above the roar of the flame. "Stay here!"

He dashed to the watering trough and immersed

himself, then soaked his handkerchief and tied it around his face. He filled his hat with water and put it on his head, letting the water run down over him. He wound a couple of wet rags around his hands, then took a deep breath and dashed into the door of the burning building. He knew he could last only seconds in this caldron. As the blasting heat hit him, his wet clothing steamed.

All around him, flames leapt and crackled. There was a roaring and splitting and breaking noise that filled his ears and blotted out any other sound and any thought. He smelled his beard singeing, felt the skin on his face almost crack in the intense heat.

Almost immediately, he saw Paul Cahill. Whoever had set the fire had tied him to a chair, had meant to burn the rancher alive. Probably Cahill had tried to escape once he was alone by trying to move the chair closer to the door. But the chair had turned over. Cahill lay helpless, his clothes had just caught on fire. Above the bellowing roar of the fire, Fargo heard Cahill scream in pain.

He raced forward through the advancing lines of fire on the floor. He pulled his hat off his head and beat the flames on Cahill's clothes. The rancher scarcely looked up, didn't seem to notice him, but appeared to have gone into deep shock. Fargo's knife was in his hand in a moment, the ropes sliced through. And then he was dragging Paul Cahill through the burning room toward the door. Just then, he heard a cracking snap and the ceiling fell in with a smash, throwing up a shower of sparks and blocking the exit to the door.

Fargo swore. The heat was intensifying. His hands were getting badly burned, he could feel them sting and his eyes spun with ghosts that danced in the smoke. His head swam. If he could just get a breath of air! But each small sip burned his lungs. Then he spotted the window on the other side of a snaking line of flame, like a thin curtain.

With a roar, he lifted Paul Cahill in his arms and plunged forward through the fire, smashing through what was left of the broken window and stumbling across the porch just as the entire roof of the ranchhouse collapsed with a shriek of falling timber and joinery. Betsy cried out when she saw them.

Fargo staggered across the yard, as Betsy followed close behind. He dumped Paul Cahill into a watering trough. It would hurt like hell but it would cool him down quick, put the flames out. Then he found another trough for himself, dipping himself in the cold water that burned more than the fire did. Yeah, he'd get some dandy blisters on his hands and cheeks, he realized. And his beard would take some time to grow back. But altogether, he was all right.

As he splashed the water over him, he heard Paul Cahill screaming in agony. Fargo knew the man was so badly burned he might not live through the night. Burns hurt worse than any other kind of wound and maybe it hadn't been so merciful to snatch Paul Cahill back from the jaws of death. But it was done now.

After his skin had completely cooled down,

Fargo raised himself, dripping out of the trough. The ranchhands were still trying to get control of the fire, to save something. But it looked hopeless. From time to time, one of them dashed over to check on Fargo, to congratulate him, or to see how Cahill was doing.

Fargo fished dry clothes out of his saddlebags and dressed. He found some bear-grease salve he'd got from a Ute medicine man and slathered it on his face and hands. It took the sting away. He carried the rest over to Paul Cahill. Betsy had helped her father out of the trough and had wrapped him in blankets. It was impossible to take off his wet clothes because they were so charred and his burned skin was tormenting him. He was shaking like an aspen leaf.

Fargo knelt down beside the man and daubed the bear-grease on his cracked lips, eyelids and face, then wherever the burned skin showed through his clothing. The burns were bad, some of the worst he'd seen. Cahill moaned, gritted his teeth, tried to keep from screaming. Betsy, the tears running down her face, held her father's head as he lay on the ground.

"Who did it?" Fargo asked when he finished.

"Hulbert."

"Bastard," Fargo muttered.

"Maybe I just—deserve to—die." Cahill's words came out haltingly between his cracked lips.

"Oh, Pa." Betsy sobbed.

"No, listen, honey. I was hardly older than you

when I killed a man. Shot him dead." Paul Cahill's eyes opened and he seemed to see very far away.

"You killed somebody, Pa?"

"In cold blood—" he continued, each word spoken seemed to torment him. "I was self-righteous—and hotheaded when I was young. But my pa—was good to me—gave me some money to set myself up in life when I left home." Cahill paused a moment as if gaining the strength to go on. "One night I found myself on board one of those fancy boats on the Mississippi. There was gambling—I gambled in those days, before I met your ma, God rest her soul. And there was a roulette wheel operator. Well, I figured out how he was cheating and I got mad because I'd lost all my money—every red cent that Pa had spent years saving to give me. This cheat had taken it all in about twenty minutes. I got so mad, I said some words, then I drew my pistol—and I—I shot him."

"Pa!" Betsy was deeply shocked.

As Fargo listened to Cahill's story, he remembered Ruby Murphy trying to find out the name of a man who had shot somebody aboard the *Lady Luck* many years before. Was that the connection? Could it be Paul Cahill?

"It was the worst sin I ever committed," Cahill said. "And I ran like a deer, jumped right off that boat into the river and swam to shore. They never caught up with me and I changed my name and came out here. I met your ma, told her the whole story, and I've spent the rest of my life trying to make a future for you. And hoping my past would never catch up with me."

He was silent for a while. The fires were dying down, the ranchhands were exhausted with the futile efforts to try to save something of the Flying C. Betsy sat hunched over her father as he stared up at the sky.

Dawn came, pale yellow, silent, and joyless. As the light gathered above, Fargo reached over and shut Paul Cahill's eyelids. Betsy's falling tears stung the back of his hand.

The ranchhands had gathered from all corners of the ranch and built a campfire by the remains of the barn. Now they stood around it, dispirited, directionless. Fargo walked over and told several of them to dig a grave for their boss. He put a couple of others on guard duty just in case Hulbert and his men should return. He sent another group to reconnoiter the herd and see what the losses were. The kid, Stevie Border, and his group had ridden in with the three hostages. Apparently, the posse had been making trouble all over the ranch, probably to distract attention so they could burn down the ranchhouse, and several of the other hands had captured more of Hulbert's men. They kept them tied up in one of the pigpens.

In the cold light of morning, the compound smoldered. Black timbers rose against the pale sky and gray ash was everywhere—on the ground and floating in the watering troughs. White smoke rose in columns in the still air. The sharp smell of char stung his nose.

By midmorning, some of the ranchhands came back to report that fully half the herd seemed to have been stolen or run off by Hulbert's men. They'd also lost five ranchhands in the gunfights. Betsy cried about the men who'd been killed.

"And, with half the herd gone, we'll be ruined," she said. "All Pa's work will be lost." She glanced at the blanket-wrapped figure, ready for burying.

"Maybe not," Fargo said. "We got six hostages altogether—and they're all Lars Hulbert's men. Hired by and paid for by Mort Murphy. Now, it seems to me that if those men on Murphy's payroll have run off half your herd and burned down your house, then Murphy is responsible too. I'll bet any court of law is going to see it that way.

"Do you think so?" Betsy was too depressed to sound enthusiastic, but he heard a glimmer of hope in her voice.

For the next few hours, they conducted a burial for Paul Cahill, lowering him into the ground under some elm trees not far from the burned-out compound. Several of the ranchhands lifted stones to mark the grave. There would be time later to get the undertaker in town to make a proper headstone. It would be a hot day, cloudless, the sun blistering. They rested for an hour, since nobody had slept all night. Then it was time to get back to work.

The ranchhouse was a blackened skeleton of charred timbers, the barn a heap of ashes, burned right down to the ground. Betsy looked broken, her shoulders sagged. Fargo put his arm around her.

"What do I do now?" she asked dispiritedly, tears streaking her cheeks.

"We'll get the other ranchers behind us," Fargo said. "They need to know what's happened here. With the support of the others, we could get this town cleaned up."

"Yes," Betsy said thoughtfully. "Al Hawkins' ranch is adjacent ours. We could ride over and let them know. Then maybe they could pass the word."

They left the ranchhands to the task of trying to salvage anything possible from the house, the storerooms, and the barn. The chickens and horses had been rounded up already and the cowpokes were trying to retrieve what was left of the Flying C stock. Fargo and Betsy rode out and headed toward Al Hawkins' ranch.

It was a relief to be galloping across the golden grasslands in the fresh air, away from the smoke and gritty odor of the burned-out ranch. The sun was high overhead. When they reached the Hawkins spread, they headed toward the ranch house, a comfortable-looking well-built house. They didn't see anybody around. Betsy called out, then dismounted and knocked at the door, but no one was home. They decided to head to the next ranch to see if Josh Smithers might be around.

They were cantering along the crest of a hill, about to head down into a cottonwood-choked ravine, when Fargo spotted a line of riders coming up the trail on the far side of the valley. He called out to Betsy, then reined in immediately, his hand on his Sharps rifle. He grasped the bridle of her red and pulled them both a few paces back over the crest of the hill so they could watch without being seen.

"Oh my God, it's Hulbert," Betsy said, panic in her voice.

"Wait," Fargo said as she started to turn about and run. "They haven't spotted us yet." He peered across the distance, his keen eyes searching for details, looking for Lars Hulbert, for anyone recognizable.

"Who are they?" Betsy breathed.

"What kind of horse does Al Hawkins have?" Fargo asked.

"A golden palomino," Betsy replied.

"How about Joe Smithers?"

"A red and white paint."

"I'm sure it's not Hulbert and his gang," Fargo said. "Looks like the ranchers. Let's ride down and meet them."

Fargo and Betsy moved their mounts to the top of the hill, waited until the distant riders spotted them and hailed them, then galloped down toward the tree-filled coulee. The ranchers got there first. As they arrived, they plunged into the shade under the tall cottonwoods. The ranchers stood in front of their horses, waiting in a line.

"Al! Joe! I'm so glad to see you!" Betsy said, jumping down off her horse and running toward them. Fargo dismounted and followed. The men's faces were stony, they didn't look at her, but Betsy didn't notice. He didn't like it. There was something wrong here, something heavy in the air. His hand twitched above his Colt. What the hell was going on? "They killed Pa! They burned the ranch!" Betsy started off, but the men didn't seem to hear her. Instead there was a sudden movement.

Five men vaulted toward him. He drew his Colt, fired, but the shot went awry and the gun was wrenched from him. He felt himself being knocked off his feet as hands groped to pin his arms. He struck out with his fist, connecting with someone's jaw. Then another blow crunching somebody's rib. Then he punched somebody in the nose and probably broke it from the sound of the man's yelp. They were sitting on him, holding him down. There was nothing he could do against five of them.

"What the hell—?" he shouted, but one of the men suddenly brought up a gag and tied it tight against his mouth.

"Al! Joe! Stop them!" Betsy pleaded. "What's going on? Don't you know who he is? There must be some mistake. Make them stop this!"

With the gag tight in his mouth, he could say nothing. He felt his arms being tied behind his back, then his legs bound together. Betsy continued to plead with the ranchers but they remained silent, their mouths set grimly. Fargo was hauled to his feet, held upright, and turned about to face the line of men.

"You double-crossing bastard," Al Hawkins said. "We finally caught up with you."

Fargo thought about the effigy in his hotel room and the warning that had been pinned to it about getting out of the county. Al Hawkins and the rest of the ranchers thought he was working for Mort Murphy.

"What are you doing!" Betsy screamed, tugging at Al Hawkins.

"Stay out of this, Miz Cahill," Hawkins snapped at her. "We asked you for help, Trailsman. And instead, you sold out on us. Sold yourself to Mort Murphy. Probably told him all about our plans too."

Fargo realized Al Hawkins had to be talking about the telegram, the one he couldn't read. The ranchers assumed he'd told Mort Murphy whatever had been in the message. He tugged at the ropes binding his hands, but they were too taut. He tried to move his jaw, get the gag loose, but it was tied tight, cutting into his mouth.

"Well, we've had enough of being double-crossed, Trailsman. And you're going to get what's coming to you." Al Hawkins turned to his saddle, picked up a coil of rope, and tossed one end over a tree branch. As he pulled, a hangman's noose snaked up into the air.

At the sight, Betsy shrieked, disbelieving.

"You're making a mistake!" she said. "Tell me what he's done! You can't do this!" She raced around from one rancher to the next, begging and pleading, half hysterical, but their faces were hard as rocks. They were convinced he was guilty of helping Mort Murphy. And since they couldn't get to Mort Murphy, who was protected by Lars Hulbert and his gang, they would come after him.

Cowards. He gritted his teeth and pulled at the ropes again to no avail.

Al Hawkins was securing the noose to the tree.

"Get him on his horse," Hawkins directed. Nine men surrounded him and lifted him onto the Ovaro, then pulled it toward the hanging noose. Fargo made sounds in his throat, trying to get Al Hawkins to let him talk, but the ranchers took no notice.

Betsy Cahill was beside herself with panic until Al Hawkins threatened to gag her too, saying it was none of her business. The noose was swinging back and forth before his eyes as the Ovaro was led forward. It came nearer and nearer. The pinto beneath him balked, not liking being surrounded by the men driving it forward. Then Joe Smithers came up on his horse and put the noose around Fargo's neck, tightening the knot.

In vain, he tried again to get them to take the gag off his mouth, to give him a chance to explain, to set them straight about what had happened. The telegram was in his front vest pocket. That would explain everything. He made noises in his throat again.

"Shut up," Al Hawkins said. "There's nothing you can say."

"Let him speak!" Betsy said.

Fargo tried to indicate with his eyes that they should look into his pocket, anything, anything to give him a chance.

"That's enough!" Hawkins said. "Hang him!"

In a moment, the nine men surrounding the

Ovaro tried to drive it forward. Fargo tightened his knees and legs around the pinto, willing it to stay put. It refused to budge as the men tugged on the bridle. Betsy was sobbing and one of the ranchers was restraining her from rushing forward. A whip was brought and one of the ranchers whipped the pinto's withers. Fargo could feel the trusty horse recoil slightly as the whip was laid hard into its flesh. The whip was probably drawing blood. Still the pinto remained stock-still.

"Try gunshot. That'll make it bolt," a man suggested.

They brought a rifle and stood just behind the pinto, then fired. The sound reverberated through the grove and the birds in the trees above called out and took flight. But the pinto barely flinched.

Betsy screamed but no one was paying her any attention.

"All right," Hawkins said. "Shoot the horse out from under him."

The man with the rifle stepped back. Fargo felt the rough rope grate against his skin and he bit into the gag again. Goddamn it. The rage welled in him but there was nothing he could do.

The man cocked the rifle, taking aim at the pinto.

"This will teach you to ignore our telegram, Trailsman," Al Hawkins growled.

"Telegram!?" Betsy screamed. "Telegram? Wait!"

There was something in her tone that made the man with the rifle pause a moment.

"Wait! I know about that! Fargo told me!"

"So what?" Hawkins said. He gestured to the rifleman to fire.

"The telegram was garbled! He couldn't read it."

Hawkins turned to face her, disbelief in his face.

"Yeah, maybe that's what he told you." He gave the signal again.

"I can prove it!" Betsy said. "It's in his front vest pocket. Please, please, look. Please don't kill an innocent man. He's trying to help us. All of us! I know it!"

Hawkins looked skeptical, but he had one of the men ride up and fish in Fargo's pocket. He found the piece of paper. Hawkins and several of the others leaned over it.

"She's right," Hawkins said. "Only thing I can read here is the word *Blackgulch*."

"See?" Betsy said. "And the telegram didn't even reach Fargo until last week in New Orleans."

Hawkins nodded slowly, and a few of the ranchers muttered to themselves, looking chagrined.

"But what about the fact that he's working for Mort Murphy?" Hawkins said. He turned to address Fargo, forgetting that he was gagged. "What do you say to that, Trailsman?"

In a moment someone had untied his gag, although they didn't take the noose off his neck.

"I saved Ruby Murphy from a bunch of ruffians who had kidnapped her off a casino boat," Fargo said. "I didn't know who the hell she was. Then I brought her to Blackgulch and Murphy gave me a reward. And that's the truth." And suddenly the whole thing made sense to Fargo. The riders who had captured Ruby Murphy were— "I guess I spoiled your plan to capture Ruby Murphy and trade her back to Mort Murphy in exchange for your ranches. Was that your plan? Because the fact of the matter is you all owe Mort Murphy. Every damn one of you is bankrupt. You gambled everything away to that crook and he's got you over a barrel."

There was a long silence. The ranchers looked down at their boots.

"Well," Hawkins said after a long silence. "We put two and two together and came up with five I guess. We thought you were working for Mort Murphy. We thought you'd told him everything."

"That's ridiculous!" Betsy said. Then she told them what had happened at the Flying C and how Lars Hulbert's men had come and burned down the ranch. Her voice broke when she told them how her father had died. "All because Pa wouldn't gamble it away, like the rest of you."

"Well, I guess it's all over," Al Hawkins said tiredly. "You see, Mort Murphy is going to call in our loans tomorrow. Tonight's the last night the casino is going to be open. He said he's giving us one more chance to win back our ranches. But tomorrow, he's going to the bank and all of us are going to be foreclosed. By tomorrow at noon, Mort Murphy is going to own the whole county. He'll be the richest man in Texas. And it's all legal. Mort Murphy's got the law on his side, as well as the sheriff and forty deputies. There's nothing we can do about it."

Fargo thought quickly and a plan, a desperate and dangerous plan, began to take shape.

"Oh yes," he said slowly. "Oh yes, I think there *is* something you can do about it."

From the first five minutes the casino opened, the faro and keno and chuck-a-luck tables were clattering with chips and dice and cards thrown down and scooped up. From the moment the ranchers poured into the open doors, the air was immediately thick with excitement, a kind of hushed expectation so different from the usual clink of liquor glasses and laughter. Tonight, the Blackgulch Gaming House was packed to the rafters with every ranch owner from the county leaning over the tables, putting down the last of hard-earned cash, every red cent not yet lost to the casino.

Mort Murphy walked grandly among the tables with Ruby on his arm, welcoming them all by name and telling them this would be their lucky night. The tall red ostrich feather in Ruby's hair fluttered as she nodded a greeting to all the men. Around the perimeter of the room stood Lars Hulbert and his deputies, especially wary and watchful tonight, their silver derringers in their hands. All the other guns were locked up tight in the case by the front door.

And, moving like a brown shadow through the crowd from table to table was the small wiry figure of a man dressed in rustic homespun and leather. To anyone who didn't know better, he looked like he'd just set his winter traps in the high mountains or gone on a buffalo hunt and had come to the big city looking for excitement and was about to lose all his money fast. But Josh Leatherberry's keen eyes were intent on the games, darting from here to there. He was trying to keep the smile off his face, but even from across the room and hidden behind one of the velvet draperies, Fargo could see the small grin at the corners.

Yes, Josh Leatherberry was having the night of his life and it was all going to plan, Fargo thought as he rested back against the wall and peered out from behind the curtain. He had been waiting there for hours and it was stuffy behind the velvet hanging. He knew he'd have to stay here quietly for some time more. But it was worth it to watch the show. His sudden reappearance in Blackgulch might raise some questions in Mort Murphy's mind, so it was better he stay out of sight for the present. As he watched the action in the casino, he thought back over the past several hours.

After telling his plan to the ranchers, Fargo had borrowed a wagon, hidden in the back under sacks of potatoes, and Al Hawkins and Joe Smithers had smuggled him into the Blackgulch Hotel. There he found Josh Leatherberry and the two of them went into action. In the late afternoon, they met the two ranchers at the casino, which—since it was Sunday—was dark and closed until eight o'clock when it would open for the night's gambling. The last night's gambling.

The two ranchers had done their chores and arrived with the boxes of Mrs. Dottie Hawkins' Fourth of July blank bullets from the Emporium. Fargo set the two to work replacing all the bullets in the derringers with blanks, while Josh Leatherberry practically flew from table to table replacing decks of cards, rebalancing the roulette wheel, exchanging the dealer's dice with pairs of his own. In an hour, they had finished. The two ranchers and Leatherberry slipped out the window while Fargo stayed behind, planning to secrete himself behind the curtain when the casino opened for business.

And now as he stood watching it was hard not to keep from laughing at the dealers' faces when the dice they used, and which they assumed to be loaded one way, came up the opposite. Al Hawkins, playing every nickel he could scrape together, was winning hands down and turning nickels into dollars into hundred-dollar chips and then to thousands, while the sweating dealer kept changing the dice to others that Leatherberry had replaced. At the roulette wheel, Joe Smithers was winning again and again.

Fargo looked across the room at Mort and Ruby Murphy, who were watching a rancher win at twenty-one. At the first couple of wins, Mort grinned widely and slapped the rancher on the back, assuming the dealer was giving the rancher some incentive to put more money into the game before cleaning him out. But then, as the rancher's chip pile grew dangerously high, Mort shot an inquiring look at the dealer, who shrugged and looked worried. Mort's brows came down and his eyes flashed angrily as the rancher continued to win, the chips piling up like turrets of a red, white, and blue castle.

Ruby noticed her brother's worry and whispered in his ear. He shook his head in bewilderment. They wandered away to watch the roulette wheel.

Joe Smithers was sitting behind a pile of cash and chips, pushing the whole pile forward on every turn of the wheel and winning every single time. Occasionally, he glanced up covertly toward the small figure in brown standing across the table from him, the man whom Mort Murphy hadn't even given the time of day to. Josh Leatherberry pulled on his left ear and Smithers put his money down on eight and doubled it. The roulette wheel operator reluctantly pushed a pile of chips toward him. Mort Murphy pulled his employee aside and was clearly berating him for letting Smithers win so much.

Then Murphy clapped Smithers on the back and, although he couldn't hear the words above the hubbub of the room, Fargo was sure the casino owner was trying to dissuade the rancher from playing any more at roulettes.

Smithers grinned at Murphy, glanced again at Leatherberry, who was stroking his chin. Smithers bet on twenty and doubled his money again. Now Mort Murphy smelled a rat. This time, he hung over the table watching Smithers' every move. When his eyes flicked toward Leatherberry, Murphy's gaze locked onto the man.

"What the hell?" he shouted above the noise.

"We got a cheater in here!" But just then, Mort Murphy was besieged by several of his dealers, who had run out of chips and money simultaneously. From all over the room, the casino waiters and employees were coming to Murphy to tell him that the poker table had gone bust and that the rancher at table seven had cleaned the house out of chips. The whole casino was collapsing, losing everywhere and running out of chips and out of cash to back them.

"What?" Murphy shouted. He looked around wildly for Josh Leatherberry, convinced that he was the source of his sudden reversal of fortune. He spotted him and pointed at him. "Get that man! Get that man!"

The jig was up, Fargo thought, stepping out from behind the curtain. It was time. He raised his Colt into the air and fired three shots. A rain of plaster fell down on the tables. Lars Hulbert and his men immediately drew their derringers.

"That man—it's Fargo! He's got a gun!" Murphy shouted. "Get him!"

Hulbert's men moved toward him, firing. But Fargo stood there smiling as the blank bullets exploded, echoing in the crowded room. He spun the Colt on his finger and holstered it as the sheriff and his men continued toward him, expecting Fargo to fall dead, expecting the ranchers would duck and get out of the way of the crossfire.

But instead, the ranchers rushed straight into the closing ring of Lars Hulbert and his posse of thugs. Their faces were disbelieving as they desperately fired their derringers again and again straight at the oncoming ranchers. Then fistfights broke out all over the room as the ranchers gave vent to their rage at being cheated for so long. Chairs and bottles flew through the air, men were thrown against walls and collapsing tables. The mirrors on the walls shattered into thousands of pieces.

Fargo looked around for Lars Hulbert, saw him duck behind the long oak bar. Fargo pushed his way through the roiling crowd and leapt over the bar, found the sheriff cowering there, and hauled the man to his feet. Hulbert's watery eyes were wide with fright as Fargo hauled off and gave him a right uppercut that nearly took his head off. Hulbert staggered backward as Fargo hit him again, sinking his left into the man's belly with such force that the breath left him and his red face turned purple. Next was a swift left that crunched into the bastard's jaw as Fargo thought of Paul Cahill being tied to a chair and his ranch house being set fire.

As Lars Hulbert jerked backward, his groping hand found the neck of a whiskey bottle. He grasped it desperately, then smashed it against the bar, broke it off to a jagged crown, and swung it in Fargo's direction. But he was too slow. A swift kick to the sheriff's left knee pitched him to the side. Lars Hulbert's head hit the huge mirror behind the bar and it cracked as the sheriff crumpled to the floor. The weblike cracks spread across the mirror and suddenly it slid down in a huge sheet and crashed, shattering in a shower of silver shards. A razor-sharp pointed sliver pierced the side of Hulbert's neck. A fountain of blood squirted upward and Lars Hulbert twitched, his hands groping at his neck, trying to pull the glass from the wound. His hands closed on nothing, helplessly. The bleeding continued, a pulsing geyser of red blood draining him of his life. Hulbert's pale eyes widened in fear as his hands lost their power to move and he shuddered a few times, then he lay still in the pool of red.

Fargo turned away. The fight was almost over and thanks to the element of surprise the ranchers had prevailed. Here and there some of the deputies and ranchers were still duking it out, but most of Lars Hulbert's men had already been tied up.

Fargo scanned the room, looking for Mort Murphy and his sister. He could see them nowhere. Goddamn. They couldn't get away. The door that led to Murphy's office stood ajar. Fargo pushed it open and found the room abandoned. Papers were strewn across the desk and in the corner, the metal safe stood open and empty. Whatever money Murphy had, he'd grabbed it and fled. Fargo swore, pushing his way back through the crowded room and out onto the empty street.

The town of Blackgulch was quiet and the stars overhead winked in the clear night. He stood listening, then thought he heard a horse's neigh from behind the casino. He ran down the alley just as two riders started toward him from the other direction, galloping full-out. It was them, all right.

The alley was narrow and the horses were coming full speed. A water barrel stood close at hand.

In an instant, Fargo climbed up on it, ready to jump them. Then one of the riders—Mort Murphy—drew a pistol and aimed it right at him. He ducked as a bullet zinged by, barely missing him. It was followed by a second. This time he felt the bullet hit his shoulder, knocking him sideways as he started to fall off the barrel, the pain radiating out of his shoulder and numbing his arm.

Hell, he was going to lose them. He gritted his teeth and jumped, jumped with every ounce of strength remaining in him as Mort Murphy's horse went galloping by. He landed half on the saddle, flailing with his one good arm, grappling with the rider. His hand grabbed Murphy's collar and they went down sideways off the horse, which galloped on. He felt the Colt slip out of his holster.

The ground came up hard and he hit his shoulder, the one with the bullet in it. He almost yelped in agony, but instead summoned his rage, let the pain well up in him to black—midnight black—anger as he rolled over. He kept his one-handed grip on Murphy and smashed the man's head against the hard-packed earth. Murphy's eyes were wide with sudden fright. He fumbled with something between them and Fargo felt the barrel of the gun jammed in his ribs. Damn it, his Colt was lying on the street several yards away. One shot from Murphy's gun and he was a dead man.

With a sudden jerk, Fargo pitched sideways just as Murphy pulled the trigger. The bullet discharged with a roar, and he felt its sting graze his side but, hell, he was alive. With his knee, he smashed Murphy's hand to the ground and he held him pinned under him, one boot on his other arm and his one good hand on his neck.

"You goddamn greedy bastard," Fargo rasped. The pain in his shoulder was awful and his arm hung uselessly. "You thought you could own this town. Well, you can't."

He heard the pounding of hooves and then Ruby Murphy was standing over them.

"Let my brother go," she said. That hard edge was in her voice. "I said get off him or I'll shoot. I'll shoot you in the back."

Fargo heard the click of a trigger. Yeah, she meant business. Reluctantly, he rolled off Murphy and got to his feet. She stood there with a small pistol in her palm. Small but deadly. That was Ruby Murphy, he thought to himself. Mort Murphy got to his feet, beating the dust out of his fancy clothes.

"Thanks, Ruby," Mort said. "So it was you rigged all my tables, Fargo. I should have figured that."

"They were already rigged," Fargo said. "We just rigged them so the other side would win." Hell, if only he had his Colt. It was lying on the street about six feet from him. His eyes flicked toward the spot. If he jumped for it, would she fire quick enough to—

But Mort Murphy saw the direction of his gaze.

"Let me do the honors," he said, bending down to retrieve Fargo's gun. "I'll shoot him with his own pistol."

Fargo leapt, hitting Murphy across the shoulders just as he grasped the Colt. And at the same instant, Ruby fired. Fargo felt Mort Murphy jerk as the bullet hit him in the side.

Mort screamed with pain as he went down. Fargo rolled and came to his feet. Ruby stood stock-still in horror with the gun in hand. In a moment, Fargo covered the distance between them and wrenched the weapon from her limp grasp. Her mouth gaped, her wide blue eyes open in disbelief. She ran to her brother and knelt beside him as he lay in the street looking up at the stars.

"No! No! Mort!" she screamed, shaking him. "Mort!" But he was already gone, his eyes blank, his expression slack.

Fargo stood over them until at last Ruby looked up at him, her pretty face twisted with grief.

"You don't understand," she said. "Our father was killed, shot down in cold blood. And so we were dirt poor, my mother and Mort and me. Mort vowed he'd find the killer. And he found out the man was a rancher in Blackgulch. Only he couldn't find out his name. So he swore he'd ruin every one of them. That way he'd punish the guilty one."

"And a lot of innocent men too," Fargo pointed out. "That was the name you were trying to find out from Sims back on the *Lady Luck*." Ruby nodded, then looked down at her brother and sobbed. "Mort was all I had."

"Well, if it's any consolation," Fargo said, "your father's killer is dead. It was Paul Cahill who did it. And he died in a fire last night."

Ruby looked up at him, taking in this information, her eyes filled with grief.

"That won't bring Mort back," she said bitterly.

"It won't bring Paul Cahill back either," he said. He glanced at the casino. "I think you should get out of town. I'll make sure your brother gets a decent burial." She nodded woodenly.

He helped her to her feet and brought her horse. He took the bag of money off the saddle, fished around in it and pulled out a fistful of large bills, several thousand dollars, he estimated, and put it into her saddlebags. It would be enough to set her up for a while.

"I'll give the rest back to the people it belongs to," he said. He helped her up, slapped the rump of her horse, and it trotted away down the street. Ruby Murphy rode it as if in a dream. He watched her disappear.

Mort Murphy's horse nosed the dead man, then wandered back toward the stable. The street was quiet but from inside the casino came the raucous sounds of celebration, of men shouting and laughing and excitedly recounting how they had won back their ranches and their futures.

He heard a sudden silence and a man shouted, "To Leatherberry!" And they all roared a toast in response. They'd come looking for him soon.

Fargo walked away, alone down the quiet street of Blackgulch, away from the garish lights and noise of the casino, past the dark windows of the storefronts. He needed to find the town doctor to fish the bullet out of his shoulder.

Then maybe he would ride out to the Flying C, he thought, check up on how Betsy Cahill was

LOOKING FORWARD!
The following is the opening section from the next novel in the exciting *Trailsman* series from Signet:

THE TRAILSMAN #199
WYOMING WILDCATS

1860, the Green River country, where raw lust leads to mayhem and bloodshed . . .

Someone was stalking him.

The big man on the pinto stallion was working his way down a steep slope choked with deadfall when the warning screamed in his mind. Skye Fargo could not say exactly how he knew. There had been no crackling of the undergrowth, no snapping of dry twigs. But he knew, just the same, as surely as he did that those stalking him were Indians.

Years of life in the raw had honed the Trailsman's instincts to a razor's edge. Where a city-bred man would see only the deep blue sky and hear only the soft sigh of the breeze and assume all was well, Fargo saw and heard telltale clues he was not alone. The flight of several spooked sparrows, for instance, had been his first inkling of impending danger. The manner in which all the small creatures in his vicinity, all the birds and squirrels and chipmunks, had gone suddenly quiet, was another factor.

Were the Indians peaceable or hostile? That was the big question. Fargo was half a day out from Fort Bridger, in country roamed by both the Shoshones and the Flatheads. Two more friendly tribes would be hard to find. But the Utes also prowled that region from time to time, and of late the Utes had been decidedly unfriendly. Not that Fargo blamed them. With more and more whites pushing into their territory, the Utes were simply protecting what was theirs.

Skirting another tangle of fallen trees, Fargo removed his hat and ran a hand through his dark hair. While doing so, he contrived to swivel his head just enough to scan the ridge he had crossed a couple of minutes ago. Nothing moved up there, but that meant little. If a war party of Utes had decided to ambush him, they would close in like bronzed specters, seldom showing themselves and making no more noise than would real ghosts.

Replacing his hat, Fargo reined to the right, toward a game trail he had spied that wound to a lush valley below. He must hurry without seeming to hurry. For if the Utes should grow aware he had detected them, they would cast stealth to the wind and converge like a pack of ravenous wolves.

His right hand drifted to within easy reach of the Colt nestled snugly in its holster on his hip. In a saddle scabbard under his right leg was a Henry, but he made no move to yank the rifle out just yet.

Nor would he resort to the Arkansas toothpick hidden in his boot until it was needed.

It was too bad, Fargo reflected, that he was not in heavy timber. His buckskins would tend to blend into the trees, making it harder for the Utes to keep track of him or fix a bead. He saw the Ovaro prick its ears and look off to the left. Moving just his eyes, he scoured the maze of deadfalls and spotted a blur of motion forty yards away. The brief glimpse had confirmed his hunch. He *was* being hunted, and the hunters were indeed Utes.

Fargo fought down a temptation to apply his spurs. Self-control was called for if he wanted to get out of the tight fix he was in with his scalp intact. To give the Utes the impression he was as green as a newborn babe, he began to hum the tune to a rowdy song popular in saloons and dance halls.

The game trail was barely wide enough for the stallion and pockmarked by the tracks of elk and deer. With the skin at the nape of his neck crawling, Fargo held the pinto to a leisurely gait. He constantly peeked out from under his hat brim at the vegetation on both sides. Chest-high weeds and brush hemmed him in, providing plenty of cover for warriors who might be crouched in waiting.

On his right the grass rustled. Fargo automatically slid his hand to his revolver but checked his draw when a rabbit bounded across the trail. He hoped the Utes had not noticed how edgy he was, or they might become suspicious.

The valley floor loomed a stone's throw away.

Fargo could not understand why the warriors had not tried to stop him from reaching it. Once he did, he could give the Ovaro its head and literally leave them in the dust. He risked a backward glance to insure they were not slinking up on him. Satisfied, but puzzled, Fargo faced front and lifted the reins. Their mistake was his salvation.

Then a mounted warrior materialized out of a dense stand of cottonwoods sixty feet ahead. Another followed, and another, until there were eight in all, eight swarthy Utes who spread out as they approached. They walked their horses, in no particular hurry, which told Fargo they were confident they had him trapped. Sure enough, when he glanced over his shoulder again, he discovered another half-dozen warriors had emerged from concealment and were fanning out to block any possible escape.

Fargo had three choices. He could fight, but as yet they had not shown hostile intent and unless they did he would not throw lead at them. He could try to run and get nowhere. Or he could do just what he did, namely, rein up and sit there as calmly as could be while they ringed the pinto.

He was encouraged by the fact they were not painted for war. Among almost all tribes it was customary for men who went on the war path to paint symbols on their own bodies and on their horses. The symbols, and the meanings attached to them, varied. Common among many tribes was a painted hand, which signified a warrior who had killed an enemy in personal combat. Slash marks were often used to signify the number of coup a man had counted.

Since these Utes and their mounts did not bear the trappings of warfare, Fargo was forced to conclude he had stumbled on a hunting party. On the one hand that was good news. But on the other, he had to question why they had seen fit to sneak up on him and box him in. Holding his right hand in front of his neck with the palm outward and his first and second fingers extended, he raised the hand as high as his head. It was sign language, specifically the sign for "friend."

The Utes halted. They were a somber lot, the frowns they bestowed on him proof that while they might not be inclined to slit his throat, they were not exactly pleased to run into him either.

A tall Ute had halted a splendid bay in the middle of the game trail, and it was this man who now addressed Fargo in thickly accented English. "We not your friend, white dog." The speaker wore fringed buckskins much like Fargo's own. He carried a lance, and had an ash bow and full quiver slung across his back. A hooked nose dominated his craggy face, and he had a cleft chin, unusual for a Ute. Equally unusual was the wide red headband he wore. Apaches were partial to headbands, as were some of the tribes of the desert country to the southwest, but it was rare to see a plains or mountain Indian wearing one.

"I have done you no harm," Fargo was quick to point out. He did not like how some of the other warriors were fondly fingering weapons. It would not take much to set them off, he reckoned. Better for him if he sheathed his horns and played the part of a perfect innocent. "Why do you treat me as an enemy?"

"You have pale skin," was the tall Ute's reply. "That be reason enough."

"It's not a man's skin that counts but what is in his heart." Fargo picked his words with care. "And my heart has always been open to the red man. I have lived among the Lakota, the Snakes, and others."

The Ute with the headband did not act impressed. Straightening, he gazed beyond Fargo, then at the ridge. "Where be your woman?"

The strange question gave Fargo pause. What did the Utes want with a white woman? While it was fairly common for the Comanches to steal white females, the Utes, to the best of his recollection, had never done so. "I don't have one," he finally admitted.

"All while men have them," the warrior said testily. "I think maybe you speak with two tongues."

Fargo had just been branded a liar. Among Indians, it was an offense worth fighting over, but he dared not provoke the tall Ute or it might set off the rest. Staying as calm as could be, he gestured at his back trail. "Your band has been following me for quite a spell, so you know I speak with a straight tongue."

The warrior's scowl deepened. "I be Red Band,"

he declared in a way that gave the impression it was a name the Trailsman should be familiar with.

But Fargo had never heard of the man, although it was easy to guess how the Ute came by the handle. "You must be far from the lodges of your people," he said, for lack of anything else to say. At that time of year the Utes were usually found over a week's hard ride to the south.

"Take us to woman."

Fargo's brow knit. What was going on here? Was the Ute playing with him? Maybe deliberately trying to provoke him into going for his gun? It hardly seemed likely. Indians did not generally look for an excuse to kill someone, as whites were prone to do. Curly wolves on the prowl liked to taunt their prey into making a grab for a gun so the killers could claim they acted in self-defense. But that hardly applied here. When Indians wanted to kill someone, they just up and did it.

"Take us to woman," Red Band repeated more sternly.

"I've already told you," Fargo said. "I don't have one."

"Take us to other woman. Any woman."

Fargo was beginning to lose his patience but he did not let it show. "Where would I find a female out here in the middle of nowhere?"

"Maybe friend's woman. Maybe settler have wife."

"I don't have any friends in these parts. And I don't know where any settlers might be living. I'm passing through, is all." It was true as far as it went. Fargo really did not know of any acquaintances or homesteaders who might be in the area, but he was not merely passing through. The commander at Fort Bridger had sent for him, and for all he knew, it might have something to do with this band of Utes and their cantankerous leader.

Red Band digested the information a few moments, then leaned over to whisper to the warrior on his right. They talked a bit, then Red Band squared his broad shoulders and declared, "You come with us. Find us woman."

There was only so much a man could take. Fargo casually shifted so his right hand was closer to the Colt, and replied, "I'm not going anywhere with you. If you want a woman so damn much, go to your village and take yourself a wife."

"I want white woman."

"Too bad," Fargo said, and slapped his legs against the Ovaro. The stallion reacted superbly, bounding forward and breaking into a gallop. They were on the Utes so quickly that none of the warriors had time to unleash a shaft or hurl a lance. Fargo flashed between Red Band and one of the others. Red Band grabbed for him but Fargo rammed a hand against the Ute's chest and sent Red Band toppling. In another instant he was past the line and racing westward, bent low over the saddle to make as small a target of himself as he could.

Yips and war whoops rent the air. The warriors

were in full pursuit, except for two who were helping their leader.

Fargo braced for a flurry of arrows but no shafts were loosed. Apparently the Utes wanted him alive, not dead. That was small consolation since their mounts appeared to be sturdy and fleet. Eluding them would not be easy. But Fargo had every confidence in the Ovaro. The pinto had saved their hides on more occasions than he could count.

With a flick of the reins Fargo sent the stallion pounding down onto the valley floor and off across it through knee-high grass. Thunder rumbled in their wake, the hammering of eleven sets of heavy hooves. Red Band and the two others were further back, Red Band having just mounted to give chase.

Fargo jammed his hat low so it would not be blown off. He had a twenty-yard lead but that was nowhere near enough. Angling toward verdant woodland that fringed the valley to the north, he rode flat out. The swish of the grass against the stallion's legs was nearly drowned out by the yells and screeches of the incensed Utes. Right away it became obvious that three of them were going to give him the most trouble. The trio had pulled ahead of the pack and were more than holding their own. One was on a roan, the other two rode sorrels.

It occurred to Fargo to pull out his rifle and shoot their horses out from under them. That is what most any other frontiersman would have done. But Fargo was not one of those who killed animals without cause. He'd met men who did, men who shot things for the hell of it, not because they were hungry or needed a hide or even because they were after trophy game. Fargo never shot anyone or anything unless it was justified.

A meandering stream appeared out of the grass, a ribbon of water barely deeper than the Ovaro's knees. Fargo flew across, water spraying every which way. On the other side was a low bank and he started up it only to suddenly feel the stallion slip and tilt wildly to the left. A glance explained why. The lower portion of the bank had crumpled under the Ovaro's weight, and now the pinto's hooves were churning at slippery dank earth instead of solid ground.

A cry of triumph was voiced by the nearest Ute, a burly warrior whose roan was the swiftest animal in the band. He closed in rapidly, narrowing the gap to fifteen yards, to ten. In his left hand he held a war club which he raised overhead.

The Ovaro gave a prodigious lunge upward and cleared the bank. Fargo did not look back again until he was almost to the tree line. The Ute on the roan was a dozen yards off, the pair on sorrels twice that. The rest of the band had lost so much distance they no longer posed a threat.

Into the forest Fargo streaked. Weaving and winding among the pines and firs, he pushed the stallion as hard as he dared. What with logs and ruts and other obstacles popping up in the blink of an eye, he had to be fully alert every single second. A single misstep might be disastrous.

For long minutes the race went on, Fargo never able to gain more than a few extra yards. The three Utes clung to him like glue, particularly the warrior on the roan, who was as fine a horseman as Fargo had ever seen. Soon it became obvious that in order to shake them Fargo must resort to something more drastic.

But what? Shooting one would arouse bloodlust in the whole band. They would not rest until they had tracked him down and had their revenge. Even if he managed to elude them, they would return to their people and tell what happened. Word would spread from their village to all the others, and before too long the whole tribe would be on the lookout for him. Every time he crossed their territory in the future, he would be taking his life in his hands.

There had to be a way to escape without spilling blood. But try as Fargo might, he could not think of how to accomplish it. He was still racking his brain when the trees thinned at the base of a hill. He started up without bothering to look closely. Too late, he saw the talus that littered the slope from top to bottom. Loose rocks and dirts spewed out from under the Ovaro as the stallion churned its legs to stay upright.

"Damn!" Fargo fumed at his own carelessness. He had blundered at the worst possible moment.

The pinto had to slow down or it would fall. Fargo picked his way with supreme care, climbing slowly and chafing at the delay, slanting to the left rather than going straight up. A fierce whoop reminded him of the Ute on the roan.

The warrior had shot from the woods, seen the pinto struggling, and hurtled to intercept it before it could get any higher. But the same talus that had nearly upended the Ovaro now had the same effect on the roan. Stones and gravel rained down from under its flailing hooves. It slipped and slid, lurching from side to side as if drunk.

Trying to ride on talus was like trying to ride on thick, slick ice. The debris that sometimes accumulated was as unstable as a house built of cards. It did not take much to send the whole mass cascading downward in a violent rocky avalanche. Seasoned riders knew to avoid talus as they would coiled rattlers.

Fargo continued to climb. Going back down would be twice as hard, and put him in the hands of the Utes. Already the pair on sorrels had arrived and were gingerly moving toward him. The warrior on the roan steadied his animal, then advanced, taking his sweet time.

The Ovaro had done this before. It knew to place each leg down as lightly as if treading on egg shells. All Fargo had to do was avoid gaps and areas he deemed especially unsafe. Every now and then stones would roll out from under them, but never enough to cause the pinto to slip. Time dragged. The hot sun baked the talus, causing rippling waves of heat to rise from the rocks and boulders. By the time Fargo was halfway to the top, he was caked with sweat.

In a flurry of crackling brush the remainder of the band reached the hill. Red Band pushed to the front and glared. "Come back!" he hollered. "I want woman!"

Fargo had never met anyone so female-hungry in all his born days. And why it had to be a white woman, he had no idea. Maybe Red Band had a personal hankering, like the mountain men and trappers Fargo had known who favored Indian women. He pressed on, paying no heed when Red Band and the rest began to scale the hill.

The Ute on the roan was doing remarkably well. The roan was like a mountain goat, moving agilely for a horse its size. It soon made up the ground it had lost. A wicked gleam lit the warrior's eyes and he eagerly fingered his war club. Presently he would be close enough to throw it, which posed a very real threat.

Fargo took a gamble. He was twenty feet below a flat crest on which a few trees stood. The talus was thinner higher up, less slippery but still treacherous. Urging the Ovaro briskly on, he sought the firmest footing, veering to avoid a cleft that would pitch them both down the hill. The Ute on the roan, venting a yelp of frustration, goaded the roan to catch up.

The Ovaro slipped, recovered its balance, and forged upward. Fargo was almost to the rim when he saw a long log to his right. A final lash of the reins, and he reached safety. Immediately vaulting from the saddle, he dashed to the log, squatted, and pushed. It would not budge. He threw his shoulder against it and it started to slide, then wedged fast. Meanwhile, the Utes steadily drew nearer. The man on the roan was fifteen feet below, the roan floundering on a patch of pebbles and dirt.

Flinging himself onto his back, Fargo wedged both of his boots against the dead pine, bunched the muscles in his stomach and legs, and heaved outward with all his might. The log shook and rolled but only a couple of inches. Gritting his teeth, he tried again. He could hear the roan clattering closer, ever closer. The sneering visage of the warrior hove into view. In another few moments the Ute would spring.

Exerting every sinew that packed his powerful frame, Fargo drove his legs against the log. It tilted, shifted, and broke free. Gaining speed, it rolled against the roan, and the horse panicked. Nickering and kicking, the animal tried to back away but in its haste it stepped on a wide flat rock that shot off down the slope. The Ute hauled on the reins in vain. Squealing in fear, the roan lost its footing, and horse and rider tumbled.

The log resumed rolling, gaining speed as it traveled, dislodging talus that flowed in its wake. As more and more boulders and rocks were dislodged, the flow became a torrent. In a twinkling the entire slope seemed to be on the move, sweeping toward the startled Utes.

Red Band shouted and motioned for his warriors

to flee, but only a few at the very bottom had any hope of evading the avalanche. Most were caught in the act of turning. Horses squealed in fright, men bellowed in fury. Swept into the swirling current of stone and earth, they were helpless to resist. One man leaped off his mount and tried to reach the side of the hill on foot before the talus reached him. He failed.

Fargo rose and forked leather. It would take the Utes a while to catch their horses and come after him. By then he would be long gone. He rose in the stirrups for a last look and saw Red Band go down. As the Ute was bowled over, he glanced up and shook a fist in impotent outrage. Fargo smiled.

In a rattling deluge the rockslide roiled to the base of the hill and spilled out over the grass. Warriors and horses were strewn about like chaff in the wind. None showed evidence of being seriously hurt, although one horse limped when it stood and one of the Utes cradled an arm that was bent at an unnatural angle.

Turning westward, Fargo left them eating dust. As soon as they were out of sight, he shut the incident from his mind. It was just one of many similar events that were part and parcel of life in the wilderness. Besides, he mused, it was highly doubtful he would ever run into Red Band again.

The summer's day was young yet, the heat of late morning soon to be eclipsed by a hotter afternoon. Fargo loosened his bandanna and pushed his hat back. Provided there were no other interruptions, he should reach Fort Bridger by nightfall.

Built on the left bank of Black's Fork of the Green River, the fort had originally been a trading post built by the famed mountain man, Jim Bridger. Old Jim and the Mormons who settled to the west of him in Utah never had gotten along, and eight years ago the Mormons had driven Bridger out, claiming he was too friendly with the Indians. Not true! Old Jim told the government. He complained that the Mormons wanted his lucrative trading post and the land it sat on for themselves. And he might have been right.

Before the government got around to doing anything about it, the Mormons rose up in arms. The Utah War, folks called it. Started because Mormon men were fond of having as many wives as an Arab sheik, and the government kept telling them, "Only one. Only one." The Army marched on Utah. So out of sheer spite, the Mormons burned the post to the ground.

Old Jim got back at them, though. He volunteered to guide the federal troops to Salt Lake City. Later, he leased the site of his trading post to the military, and Fort Bridger was erected.

Nowadays the post was a vital link in the chain of forts that crisscrossed the frontier. It was a major supply depot for troops further west. It helped to guard the Overland Land. Last of all, but most important, it helped to keep the Utes in line.

Fargo had been there before, and not much had

changed since his last visit. From a spine of land he surveyed the broad green valley in which it was located. The Green River was aptly named. Along its fertile banks many of the old-time rendezvous were held by the hardy beaver trappers who once roamed the mountains in search of prime peltries. Above the high walls of the fort fluttered a flag. To the northwest a dozen lodges had been set up by Indians who had ventured to the post to trade.

No homesteads were in evidence, and for that Fargo was grateful. In his estimation, far too many settlers had flocked westward in recent years. Already cabins and sod houses dotted the landscape from Texas clear to Canada. Denver had recently been incorporated as a *city*, and other towns in the central Rockies were flourishing. For someone who loved the pristine wilds as much as Fargo did, the influx of Easterners was a sorry state of affairs.

The gates were wide open. Bored sentries lounged on either side, neither giving Fargo more than a casual scrutiny as he entered. Tired troops drilled on the parade ground. In front of the sutler's half a dozen Shoshones were haggling over furs they had brought in.

Fargo made straight for the headquarters building. In front of it two small covered wagons were parked. As he swung around the tongue of the first one to reach a hitching post, a pair of slender figures blundered directly into his path and he had to haul on the reins to keep from colliding with them.

"Watch where you're going!" the tall one bawled.

"Don't you have eyes?" snapped the other.

They were women. The taller was a shapely brunette whose piercing green eyes shone with vitality. Her companion was a petite but amply endowed blonde whose blue eyes were as icy as the craggy heights of Long's Peak. Finding two such luscious females at the post was surprising enough. But even more shocking was to see them both in men's clothes, pants and flannel shirts and all.

"Look at him, Diana," the brunette sniffed.

"Sitting there gaping like the dumb brute he is," responded the other. "How typical of a man, Hester."

Fargo was too flabbergasted to comment.

Just then a man in uniform stepped from the headquarters building, saw him, and came over, offering a hand. "Let me guess. You must be the scout we sent for, the Trailsman. The dispatch said you would be riding a big pinto stallion. I'm Major Edward Canby, Tenth U.S. Infantry, the one who sent for you. It's an honor, sir, to make your acquaintance."

"Major," Fargo said, tearing his gaze from the two lovelies. "They told me at Fort Laramie that I had to get here as quickly as I could. What's the trouble?"

Major Canby blinked. "Why, none whatsoever. Didn't they tell you why you were needed?" He pointed at the women. "We'd like you to guide these two ladies into Indian country."